THE
CAVES OF KLYDOR

THE
CAVES OF KLYDOR

DOUGLAS HILL

A MARGARET K. McELDERRY BOOK

ATHENEUM   1985   NEW YORK

One for Daryl and Lynn

LIBRARY OF CONGRESS CATALOGING IN PUBLICATION DATA

Hill, Douglas Arthur.
  The caves of Klydor.

  "A Margaret K. McElderry book."
  "An Argo Book."
  Summary: Soon after being exiled to the planet
Klydor, five young people begin to suspect that
their struggle for survival is somehow linked to the
rebel uprising against the Earth's harshly
authoritarian government.
  [1. Science fiction]
PZ7.H5493Cav   1985   [Fic]   84-20481
ISBN 0-689-50320-2

Printed and bound by Fairfield Graphics
Fairfield, Pennsylvania
Designed by Christine Kettner
First American Edition

Contents

1

The Badlands

The broad river, more than a kilometre across, swept smoothly along under the hot orange sun of the planet Klydor. The water was clouded with reddish-brown silt, its dark surface glistening greasily. On either side, the banks rose in low, rugged slopes, formed mostly from bare rock, creased and ridged and broken. Here and there the surface of the rock was softened by a patch of grey-green turf, or a stand of dark brush. But the river seemed to be the only moving thing under that sun. No creatures moved across the harsh terrain, no breath of wind stirred the brush. The land lay silent and still, as if asleep and dreaming some unknown alien dream.

But then the silence and the stillness were disturbed. A strange floating object came into view around a bend in the river. It was a raft, made from slim poles held together by stout vines. And on the raft rode five beings who seemed totally out of place in that wild landscape, and yet somehow totally at home.

Five human beings. Five young people from Earth, who had been on Klydor for only a few weeks, yet who had come to feel that it was theirs, in a way, since they had no doubt that they were the only ones of their kind on the planet.

They were all between the ages of sixteen and eighteen, and they all wore similar clothing—plain, dull-brown tunics and trousers. Each of them carried small backpacks, made from torn strips of cloth. But otherwise they were very different, in surprising ways.

On opposite sides of the raft sat two boys, one small and wiry, with skin the colour of old ivory, and the other tall, rangy and coffee-coloured. The heads of both were entirely hairless, with a ridged scar on each naked scalp that formed a letter—J on the smaller one, R on the tall one. Each of them also had a small letter s, made of some silvery metal, embedded in the skin of his forehead.

The boys held flat lengths of wood, roughly trimmed to make crude paddles. Equally crude but effective-looking spears lay on the raft within easy reach of their hands. And a similar spear lay beside a girl who sat next to the smaller of the two boys. She was short and sturdily built, with black hair that bristled up from her head like wire. The skin of her face was darkened with what looked like black paint, while the rest of her exposed skin, on her hands and neck, was reddened and peeling from sunburn. And her eyes were squeezed nearly shut, as if she found the sunlight painful.

The other two in the group, a boy and a girl, seemed ordinary by comparison. The boy, sitting at the rear of the raft with another paddle, was broad-shouldered and deep-chested, with a thatch of dark red hair. His stockiness made him look a little overweight—until, as he paddled, his tunic tightened over the mounded roll of solid, powerful muscles. The weapon at his feet was not a spear, but an even more primitive wooden club, heavy and knotted.

At the front of the raft knelt the fifth member of the group, a slim girl with tawny blonde hair and intelligent grey eyes, who carried a hand-made knife at her hip. She was carefully studying the river ahead of the raft, and the rocky slopes of the banks, with a small frown creasing her brow.

"I think the current's speeding up," she said.

"Good," said the smaller of the two scarred boys lightheartedly. "Get us outa here faster. What did you call this place, Samella?"

The blonde girl, whose name was Samella Connel, turned her frown towards him. "I've told you twice, Jeko. Badlands. It's what places like this are called back where I grew up."

"Good name for a bad place," muttered the black-faced girl.

Jeko grinned. "Ol' Heleth doesn't like all this sunshine," he announced. "What you could do, Heleth, you could empty your backpack and pull it over your head. Then you'd be outa the sun and we wouldn't hafta look at your face . . ."

Heleth clenched her fists and glowered. "You want to go for a swim, yeck-mouth?"

"Don't hurt him, Heleth," said the taller of the scarred boys, with laughter in his deep voice. "We might need him."

"Sure," Heleth growled. "For bait, if we go fishing."

They all laughed, but the small frown had still not left Samella's brow. "What do you think, Cord?" she asked. "The river's definitely faster."

All of them glanced round at the red-headed boy, whose name was Cord MaKiy. They were not looking for orders, since there were no leaders in their group. But Cord was a Highlander, one of the tough, untamed folk from the bleak mountains of northern Britain. He knew about wilderness survival, and the other four deferred to that knowledge.

"Let's keep going," Cord said. "There's no telling what kind of things we might meet on land, in those rocks. We're safer out here—and getting through the badlands faster, like Jeko said."

"Don't want to move *too* fast," the tall boy put in quietly.

"Rontal's right," Samella said. "If we hit rough water, it could wreck the raft."

"Maybe," Cord replied. "But we haven't hit any yet. We'll get off the river if we have to."

"If we can," said Rontal, the tall boy. But he agreed without demur when the others decided to go along with Cord's suggestion, and stay on the raft for a while longer. To all of them, the badlands—all the steep-sided ridges and gullies of bare and broken rock—seemed more and more forbidding. And they were grateful to the broad, silty river for hurrying them through that region.

11

But they became less grateful, some distance farther on. The current had continued to speed up, rushing the raft along alarmingly, and many sudden swirls and eddies appeared on the water's surface, possibly created by rocks below the surface. Cord needed all his startling strength, leaning on his paddle to steer the raft, to keep it from spinning like a dry leaf on that rushing torrent. And though they might all have plied their paddles to fight the current and get the raft to shore, there was no longer any point in doing so. The banks had become higher and closer to the vertical—sheer cliffs of grim grey rock, offering no level areas for landing.

As they rounded another tight bend, the river seemed to leap ahead even faster. Cord was mentally calling himself every name he could think of, for having talked the others into staying on the increasingly dangerous waterway. But then all thought fled from his mind for an instant, and his knuckles whitened as his hands clenched on the paddle.

The sound from ahead of them was like the rumbling growl of some impossibly enormous beast. Heleth, Rontal and Jeko turned towards Cord, questioningly. But it was Samella, pale beneath her tan, who answered the unspoken question, in a tense murmur that was almost drowned by the swelling noise ahead.

"White water," she said. "Rapids."

Cord nodded miserably. But there was no time for him to say anything, even if his words could have been heard. The river flung them forward, around another bend, and they saw it. A seemingly endless stretch of foam and froth and turbulence, with sharp edges and points of rock rising wetly out of it, like claws, waiting to rend and tear at their flimsy craft.

Then they were plunging into the midst of it. The raft leaped and bucked on the seething water, and the river roared as if in greedy triumph, muffling Jeko's wild reckless yell. Cord drove his paddle deep, muscles bunching as he forced the raft to swerve away from a looming fang of rock. Then he was powering his paddle in the opposite direction, the others paddling as furiously, to avoid another cluster of craggy deadliness. Time and again they fought the grip of that terrible current, swinging back and forth, in and out among the barriers of rock.

Then the river's roar grew impossibly louder, and Cord froze into stillness as he saw roiling, foaming disaster rushing towards them.

A waterfall.

Before they could try to brace themselves, the river swept the raft to the edge of the fall and hurled it over. The teenagers were flung away from it, hurtling through the blinding spray, deafened by the river's maddened bellow. It was only a low fall, less than twenty metres, but it seemed that they were dropping through the spray for many minutes. Then the water rose up and struck them like a sheet of granite. They sank deep beneath the surface, where the furious water seemed to grow a thousand hands that clutched at them, dragging them deeper.

Cord's lungs were bursting, the weight of his clothes and backpack were holding him down, and raw panic battered at his mind. Yet by instinct he kicked and flailed, trying to force his way to the surface. Then, as if by some strange whim, the river stopped clutching him and flung him away. He shot upwards, in the grip of a different swirl, and burst through the surface like a suddenly released cork.

Air had never tasted so sweet to him as he filled his aching lungs. He flung water from his eyes, looked around, and almost sank again in sheer surprise.

He was in the midst of a broad, calm stretch of water, like a fair-sized lake. It was as if the river had used up all its energy in the rapids and the waterfall, and had now spread itself out—within a low basin, several kilometres across—to laze for a while. But even more importantly, the raft was bobbing serenely on the surface, unharmed, only a few metres away. And around it, at varying distances, a number of objects were visible on the glistening water—including his four friends.

The relief that filled Cord was as sweet as that first lungful of air. They had all survived. The river had tormented them briefly, but let them live. And Cord was almost laughing as two strokes of his powerful arms brought him to the raft. He heaved himself up on to it, in time to reach down and lift Samella up as if she were weightless.

She was coughing weakly, but she managed a crooked grin of thanks. Then Cord turned to lend Rontal a hand, for the tall boy had been swimming around, gathering up the floating objects—two of their paddles, Cord's club, and all three of the wooden-hafted spears.

"We do get lucky," Rontal grunted, as he pulled himself on to the raft.

"Seems so," Cord said, and he and Samella grinned. Then the three of them turned to look at Jeko and Heleth, and the grins faded.

Jeko was swimming strongly, but slowly, because one wiry arm was supporting Heleth. The black-faced girl's head was lolling, with a ribbon of bright blood trailing through the dark hair on her temple.

"Musta hit her head on a rock, underwater," Jeko said as he reached the raft. "She's okay—just kinda dazed. Give a hand."

Cord reached down, gripped Heleth under the arms, and hoisted her up as easily as he had lifted Samella. As he did so, Rontal stretched a hand towards Jeko.

But Jeko did not take the hand. Around the raft, beneath the water's surface, the lake had suddenly begun to seethe. And there was an almost comic look of open-mouthed surprise on Jeko's face—just before his head vanished beneath the dark water.

Cord was still burdened with Heleth and could only stare with

14

shock, for a half-second, at the spot where Jeko had been. Before he could gather his wits, Rontal took one blurring stride and split the water in a clean dive, a spear in his hand.

The underwater turbulence continued, though nothing could be seen in the murky depths. Even so, Cord let go of Heleth and hurled himself from the raft after his friends. But he was not needed. The two scarred hairless heads reappeared almost instantly above the surface—and Rontal half-flung Jeko on to the raft. Then he and Cord scrambled up after him, Rontal still gripping his spear.

"Some kinda little fishes down there," Rontal gasped, as Jeko choked and spluttered. "All head and teeth. Lotsa them fastened on to Jeko, dragged him down."

"I'm okay," Jeko said with a cough, as Samella bent over him. "Took me by surprise. No damage."

Cord saw the ragged tears in the tough material of Jeko's trousers, the indentations of small teeth on his boots. "Lucky they were *little* fish."

"Like Rontal says," Samella replied with a wry smile, "we do get lucky."

"Not all of us." Heleth was sitting up, holding the side of her head and scowling. "It's Jeko I got to thank, not luck."

"Any time," Jeko said. Then he grinned an impish grin. "I'm just glad I didn't hafta give you the kiss of life."

The raft rocked as he dodged away from the cuff that Heleth aimed at him. But Heleth was giggling, and then they were all laughing with the release of tension, the pleasure in knowing that they were alive and safe and unharmed.

As the laughter died down, Cord began to shrug out of his backpack. "Let's see what damage the water has done," he said.

The others watched Cord with some anxiety as he drew, from his pack, a small square case of dark metal. The five of them had

15

salvaged a few items from the wreckage of the spaceship that had brought them to Klydor. But none of the items was as precious to them as that little metal case.

It contained a special data-storage computer, known as GUIDE, who had come to be almost a sixth member of their group. All of them were as worried as Cord about the effect the water might have had on GUIDE.

Cord looked at Samella. "You think he's all right?"

Though she was highly skilled with electronics and computers, Samella could only shrug. "Only one way to find out." She leaned forward. "GUIDE? Are you damaged?"

"Thank you for activating me." The little computer was voice-activated, and its usual reply, in its soft metallic voice, seemed entirely normal. "I have suffered no damage."

The others sighed with relief, and quickly checked the contents of their own packs—mostly spare clothing, a partial medi-kit and small containers of food concentrate, brought with them from their wrecked ship.

"Medi-kit's okay, and so's the food," Rontal announced.

"If it wasn't," Jeko said with a grin as they replaced their packs, "we could always catch us some of those toothy little fish."

"You go ahead," Heleth told him. "Maybe they'll be poisonous."

As Cord placed GUIDE in his backpack again, and pulled it on, Samella leaned towards him once more. "GUIDE, do you have any information about this region of Klydor?"

They all waited hopefully. At one time the little computer had contained an enormous range of facts about the planet. But many of its miniaturized data banks had been damaged or destroyed in the ship's crash-landing. So now GUIDE's knowledge of Klydor was patchy and incomplete.

And in this case, it was worse than incomplete. "I retain no data about this region," the soft computer voice told them.

Rontal grunted. "So we find out the hard way."

But Samella had not given up. "Is there *nothing* you can tell us?" she asked GUIDE. "About life-forms or anything?"

"I have only one item of data concerning this region," GUIDE replied, "which I have acquired since you activated me."

Cord looked startled. "You mean just now? What could you learn out here on a raft?"

"My sensors have picked up a faint electronic signal," GUIDE told them quietly, "from deeper within this region."

The five teenagers went very still, as the computer's voice continued.

"It is a signal that could only be emitted by the operational computer of a spacecraft. An Earth spacecraft."

2

Death from the Depths

ColSec.

The word grated in Cord's mind, charged with menace like the syllables of some evil spell. And he had no doubt that the word, the hated name, was also uppermost in the thoughts of the others.

They had talked about it tensely, before Cord and Rontal took up the two remaining paddles and began to move the raft across the lake. All of them knew what the strange signal had to mean. GUIDE said it came from a ship from Earth. And no one on Earth owned spaceships—except ColSec.

Colonization Section. ColSec. The hated enemy. The ruthless, callous people who flung teenagers into exile on alien planets, not caring whether they lived or died. ColSec was on Klydor.

Cord and his friends had expected a visit from a ColSec ship eventually, but not so soon. They had not got round to planning what they would do when the enemy finally arrived. Now, taken by surprise, they still had no plan. There were too many questions that needed answering—mainly, how many people the ship carried, what kind of people they were, and what they were doing on Klydor.

Cord had no illusions about ColSec. There was little chance that the visit was being made out of concern. There was only a slim chance that it was an accidental visit, which had nothing to do with the teenage exiles. In any case, they needed more information.

As the raft drifted slowly on, their mood was one of bitter

fury—because of what ColSec was and what it had done to them, and because it had now intruded on the world that they had come to see as their own. But even within their anger they did not neglect the watchful caution that had seen them through so many dangers on Klydor.

The sheer cliffs were behind them now, but around the lake the land still rose in steep, rugged slopes, quiet and still as ever. And the five of them steadily watched those slopes, in silent wariness. The bumps and folds of rock offered many hiding places for possible watchers, and the raft was totally exposed in the middle of the lake. If those possible watchers were unfriendly . . .

With both anger and anxiety growing within him, Cord thrust his paddle deep, forcing the raft ahead more swiftly. And as he paddled, and watched, he brooded—about ColSec, and the presence of a strange spaceship on Klydor.

In the sixteen years of his life in the remote Highlands, Cord had known almost nothing of spaceships, or any high technology, or most other aspects of life in the outside world. But he had known at least about ColSec—that it was one section of the monstrous Organization that held all Earth in its crushing grip. It was not until he had left Earth—unknowingly, unwillingly—that he had learned more details, mostly from Samella, about the unhappy world from which he had been exiled.

The Organization had taken control, he learned, during the years of chaos after the "Virus Decades", which had wiped out much of humanity and wrecked human civilization. The Organization had restored some of that civilization, but at a terrible price. It controlled humanity as if people were mindless robots, demanding total obedience of them, allowing no dissent. Ordinary people lived in dull drudgery and poverty, never daring to question or complain, for fear of the brutal Civil Defenders, enforcers of the Organization's laws.

19

The people were poor because those areas of Earth where they could still live had lost nearly all their resources and natural wealth. But the Organization was rich, for it had new sources of wealth. Colonization Section went out among the stars, to find other worlds with resources to exploit. And on those worlds it planted colonies—choosing some special people to be the colonists.

There had been a few courageous groups, now and then, that had dared to resist the Organization. Some had even moved into open rebellion, only to be instantly and savagely crushed. But other groups chose merely to reject the society created by the Organization, to make their own lives in areas that were too bleak or too ruined to interest the Earth's cruel masters.

One such group, the Highlanders, retreated into the free, barbaric ways of earlier centuries, among their rainswept mountains. Others, like Samella's family, found freedom of a kind on the arid dustbowl of the American prairies. Such people were usually left alone, for it was not worth the effort to clear them out, and they offered no threat to the Organization's grip on the rest of the world.

But different groups sought their freedom in the heartlands of the Organization—in the ruined, impoverished centres of great or once-great cities. These were the juvenile gangs, with their strange garb, their manic music, their knowledge of survival in the urban jungles. The gangs obeyed no rules but their own. They lived by their wits, by violence and petty crime, and sneered at the "straight" world of dull misery and fear.

Jeko and Rontal had spent their lives in a large and powerful gang called the Streeters, wild young swaggerers who made their home in Limbo, the crumbling heart of a mighty city in the American Segment. And Heleth had grown up in Britain as one of a notorious gang called the Vampires, who were the undisputed rulers of the Bunkers, a vast complex of underground passages beneath the desolate ruins of Old London.

The strength of the gangs was a major annoyance to the Organization. Yet the gangs could not be crushed, as a direct rebellion could. The Civil Defenders were unable to overcome the young outlaws in the tangled urban ruins that they knew better than anyone. So the Organization devised a partial solution.

Colonization Section—ColSec—needed colonists to plant on the alien worlds that were to be exploited. And any youthful offenders that were captured were ready-made colonists. They were usually tough enough to deal with the hardships and dangers of other planets. And if they failed to survive, they were expendable. There were always plenty more to take their place.

Cord and Samella had not belonged to outlaw gangs. Cord had been arrested after a berserk explosion of rage, when his dying uncle had been turned away from a clinic because of a lack of money. Samella had been falsely accused and convicted of theft by the computer firm where she had worked in near-slavery. So they went into exile, too, with ten other teenagers, to live or die on the planet Klydor.

As it was, some of them did die, at the very beginning. The spaceship developed a malfunction, and crash-landed on Klydor. The crash killed six of the twelve, and wrecked the ship, destroying most of the supplies, weapons and equipment that they should have used to build their colony. But Cord, Samella, Rontal, Jeko and Heleth survived the crash.

And so did a sixth youth—a crazed, highly trained killer who called himself the Lamprey. His presence was a constant danger, as were other presences in the forest where they had crashed. Days of terror and violence had followed, as the young exiles encountered weird telepathic trees, giant flesh-eating worm-monsters and shadowy, deadly aliens. At last they fought a desperate final battle against these enemies, after the aliens had gruesomely slaughtered the Lamprey. And then the five survivors wasted no time in leaving that frightening forest.

21

They left with a definite aim in mind. It was inspired by Cord, out of an unquenchable flame of hatred that he felt for ColSec. Despite having few supplies and almost no equipment except GUIDE, they *wanted* to build a colony on Klydor—not for ColSec but for themselves. They wanted it to be their own world, where they could live in peace and freedom.

So they began an exploration. From the forest they descended into an enormous valley of soft turf and rich vegetation, which was bisected by a broad, winding river. The river had speeded their progress, once they had made their raft from slim, light trees that grew along the banks. And before long the river had carried them on into much rougher country—the badlands, the region of low craggy hills and bare rocky ridges, broken up by twisting ravines and gullies.

Through all the days of their travelling, the five had never forgotten one continuing threat, which cast a shadow on their future. It was ColSec policy to send out inspectors, after some months, to see if a new group of colonists had survived. If the five friends were going to keep Klydor for themselves, they knew that one day they would have to deal with those inspectors, who could call on the full power of ColSec and the Civil Defenders.

When they began their exploration, that day of confrontation had seemed a long way ahead. But now it had arrived, unexpectedly. There was an Earth spaceship on Klydor, which had to be a ColSec ship. It might have brought the inspectors, arriving early for reasons of their own. Or it might be there for quite different, but equally threatening, reasons.

As the raft slowly drew closer to the far shore of the lake, Cord was growing more and more uneasy. His mind was filled with dire imaginings about the mysterious ship, and its occupants. And a chill was prickling his spine as he studied the rocky slopes at the water's edge. The stillness seemed to hang over the expanse of water, and the rugged land, like an invisible cloud, more heavy and oppressive than the heat of the sun.

"I don't like this," Rontal muttered.

"Nor do I," Samella said quietly. "It feels like we're being watched."

That was the feeling, Cord thought. Some animal instinct, some ancient sixth sense, was warning them all that eyes were studying them from an unseen hiding place.

He dug his paddle deeper into the water. Ahead, the dark lake lapped against a nearly level shelf of rock, at the foot of one of the slopes. It was the most likely landing place. But at that moment the raft jolted beneath them, as if it had grazed against some underwater obstacle. Cord peered down at the silty surface, seeing nothing. The raft jolted again, more strongly.

"Hold it!" Cord said. His muscles swelled as he used the flat of his paddle to halt the raft, so it would not tear itself apart on an unseen rock. The others were also peering at the water, and Rontal thrust his paddle down to probe for the obstacle. Then he halted, as they all went rigid with sudden tension.

Less than five metres from the raft, the water began suddenly to heave and seethe. And out of that disturbance, in a surge of oily bubbles, a monstrousness arose.

It was a creature that looked like a disc—a huge disc, wider than the raft. It was thinner at the edges than at the centre, and from one side to the other ran a long, narrow slit. The whole thing was covered with grey-black hide, wrinkled and lumpy. Towards the front, small knobs jutted out like blunt horns. Then, from within the knobs, wet objects that had to be eyes slid slowly out, to glare at the raft with unblinking balefulness.

The five humans stared back at the monster with horror. At the same time, Cord slid a hand forward to grasp his club, the others reached to take up their spears, and Samella slipped the knife from her belt.

The raft rocked slightly with their movement, and as it did so the water rippled briefly behind the huge, grotesque disc. Then Cord saw that the disc was merely the creature's head. Behind it, stretching for several metres, was a flat and powerful body, sprouting several thick fins that ended in evilly hooked claws.

"Looks just like the little fish that bit me," Jeko muttered.

"Guess they were the babies," Rontal said through clenched teeth. "This here's the grandaddy."

Cord's eyes remained fixed on the monster. As he watched, the narrow slit that ran the width of the disc-head gaped slightly open—and Cord realized that it was an enormously wide mouth. From its centre, a black tongue protruded. It was as thick as a sturdy rope, tapering to a point that was barbed like a fish-hook.

Almost too swiftly for the eye to follow, the tongue shot forward, spearing through the air towards Rontal. With equal speed, the tall Streeter flung up his paddle, to block the frightful barb. The point splintered the flimsy wood—then the tongue drew sharply back, jerking the paddle from Rontal's hand. For a second more, the ghastly eyes, rising out of the horn-like knobs, glared at the raft.

Then the slit mouth opened farther, like the parting of an oyster shell. Inside that massive mouth was a small forest of overlapping, dagger-sharp fangs.

Without warning, the powerful body churned the water to foam. Fanged mouth still gaping wide, the horror charged at the raft.

Rontal flung himself back, colliding heavily with Heleth and Jeko on the other side of the raft. Where he had been, the side of the raft disappeared, as the monster's jaws closed on it with a terrifying, crunching impact. The raft heaved and leaped—and in a flailing tangle of arms, legs and spears, Rontal and the other two were hurled into the murky water.

In the frantic half-second before the monster struck, Cord had dropped his paddle and fastened his left hand in a fierce grip on the vines that held the raft together. He kept that grip, the sinews of his arm as taut as cables, while the raft threshed under the monster's attack. Then he brought his club whistling through the air with stupefying force, smashing it down on two of the knobs that held the creature's eyes.

Slowly, the creature drew back. The rest of its eyes still glared malevolently, and the vast fanged mouth champed at fragments from the shredded side of the raft. Cord glanced anxiously around and saw that Samella had also clutched the vines of the raft and was dragging herself up from where she had been half-flung into the water. The other three, splashing wildly, heaved themselves with frantic haste back onto what was left of the raft. Yet there was no panic in their eyes, and they had not lost hold of their spears.

The monster continued to eye them, and Cord curled his fingers more tightly around the vines, hefting the club in his other hand. The remains of the raft shifted slightly as the others found their balance and also gripped the vines.

"C'mon, yeck-face," Heleth muttered, scowling at the monster. "You'll eat spears 'fore you eat us."

As if in response, the creature's terrible mouth gaped wide again. Its body twitched, stirring the water, as it prepared for another surging attack.

But that attack was never made.

From somewhere on the rocky slopes above the raft, a narrow beam of dazzling light lanced through the air. The monster's head seemed to erupt in a fountain of purplish blood, as the laser beam sliced lethally into its flesh.

3

The Spaceman

The remains of the raft swung towards the narrow shelf of rock at the lake's edge. The teenagers hurled themselves onto the rock, and lay for a moment gasping like netted fish, recovering from the after-effects of that ghastly attack and the unbelievable last-minute rescue. Then at last they raised their heads to peer up at the rocky slope above them.

The laser weapon had been fired from somewhere on that slope, Cord knew. But there was no sign of movement, no one visible on the slope. Whoever had saved them was mysteriously remaining hidden.

Jeko's wry voice broke the silence. "Never thought I'd want to shake the hand of some fell' from ColSec."

"They don't seem to want you to," Samella said, scanning the slope intently.

"Why don't they show themselves?" Heleth demanded.

"Let's go find them," Rontal said calmly, "and ask."

They began to scramble up the slope, spreading out to cover as much ground as they could in the climb. But they had gone only a few metres when they were halted—by the sound of another human voice.

"Don't come any closer," the voice said.

Cord and the others looked up, startled. A man had materialized, as if rising from the rock itself, on the slope several metres above them. He held a laserifle cradled in one arm, almost casually, yet its tapering muzzle was aimed down the slope, at the teenagers.

The man seemed to be in his late thirties, compact and lean. He wore a silvery jumpsuit, and had close-cropped fair hair and blue eyes that were cool and expressionless.

"Kids," he said, as if talking to himself. "So they've started a colony here. I should have expected it."

The others looked up at him suspiciously, until Samella finally broke the silence. "We have to thank you for shooting that creature."

The man nodded briefly, his eyes sweeping over the crude weapons that the teenagers held. "You can get into trouble," he said dryly, "wandering around like primitives. Where's your colony, and where are the rest of you?"

"There is no colony—yet," Cord said. He was developing a dislike for the man's tone. "We're all there is. Our ship crashed, a few weeks ago. The others were killed, and we lost most of our supplies."

The man's expression did not change. But Cord detected a faint flicker—sympathy? disappointment?—in the depths of the blue eyes.

"How about saying who you are?" Heleth said. Her glower showed that she, too, was growing annoyed.

The man gave her a wintry half-smile that held no trace of humour. "Who I am is no concern of yours. You won't see me again. I'm . . . just passing through."

Then Samella surprised them all. She had been studying the man, her eyes narrowed slightly. "I *know* who you are," she said. "I saw something about you on the vid once. You're Bren Lathan— ColSec's top space explorer."

Cord stiffened at the mention of the hated name of ColSec, and felt the stir as the others reacted. But he did not miss the flare in the man's eyes, nor the twitch of the hand that held the laser gun.

"You've got a good memory, girl," he said coldly to Samella. "Makes me wish I'd left that monster alone."

Samella blinked, shocked at the harsh words. And hot anger flamed within Cord. He took a half-step forward, up the slope—but the rifle's muzzle swung towards him, and the blue eyes above it were as icy as an Arctic morning.

"Stay where you are," Lathan snapped. "The smart thing for me would be to kill you where you stand. Don't tempt me."

Cord halted, glaring. And the laserifle swung to one side, where Jeko was crouched and snarling and Rontal was half-raising his spear for a throw.

"Don't do it," Lathan told them. "You'd be dead before you took a step."

Samella had turned pale, but her voice was steady. "Why should you kill us? Because we know who you are? What's so secret about that?"

"Yeah," Rontal growled. "You're a big famous hero from ColSec. Lots of folk know who you are."

The chill blue eyes grew flinty. "Not from ColSec, sonny," Lathan said. "I'm a freelance. I find planets—I found this one, a few years back—and ColSec pays me. But I'm my own man."

"Then what," Samella asked quietly, "are you afraid of?"

Lathan glanced at her, with another half-smile. "Afraid? You're a perceptive girl. But let's just say I'm . . . careful. For reasons of my own, I don't want to advertise my presence on Klydor."

Jeko snorted. "Who'd we tell? The fish?"

"You're supposed to be colonists, boy," Lathan said coolly. "A few months from now, the ColSec inspectors will be here to check on you."

"So you'd shoot us down," Cord said through gritted teeth, "to keep us from telling them about you."

Lathan looked at him bleakly. "No," he said. "That's their way—the Organization's way. Not mine. I just want you to stay away from me—and don't try to follow me." Another fleeting emotion showed itself in the chill blue eyes, and Cord thought that it looked oddly like sadness. "There's nothing I can do for you," Lathan went on. "But if you're grateful for having your lives saved, you can repay me by forgetting you saw me." The expressionless gaze swept over them all again. "If you're still alive when the inspectors get here."

"We've got by so far," Rontal growled.

"Right," Heleth said angrily. "Don't worry about us. Or about the inspectors. We don't like ColSec any more'n we like you. We wouldn't tell them which way was up. So you can get on back to your ship and get off our world."

This time, Lathan's half-smile was more of a grimace. "*Your* world? I suppose it is. And I wish I could get off. But my ship . . . blew up, in space. I landed here in an escape module. One-way trip."

The teenagers stared at him disbelievingly. "Then whose ship is it?" Jeko blurted.

The words shattered Lathan's icy calm. His face twisted with what looked like fear, and the laserifle quivered alarmingly in his hand. "What are you saying?" he demanded. "What ship?"

"There's an Earth ship somewhere in the badlands," Cord said bluntly. "We came looking for it."

Lathan swung to face Cord, eyes blazing. "How could you know?"

Cord hesitated, unwilling to tell the stranger everything. But then Lathan's eyes shifted to Cord's backpack. He saw the glint of metal, and the half-smile reappeared.

"So you salvaged the GUIDE computer from your shuttle," he said. "And it's picked up a signal from a ship." The smile became a grin, which looked almost happy. "Now I'm glad I saved you from that monster. A GUIDE is just what I need." He extended a hand, commandingly. "Let's have it."

Cord hunched his shoulders, glaring. "You'll have to come and get it."

Lathan's smile faded, and his eyes went cold again. "I may not be an Organization killer, kid," he said sharply. "But I'm not playing games. Give me the GUIDE, or I'll take it off your corpse."

"Give it to him, Cord," Samella said quickly. "He's frightened of something, and desperate—and he means it."

Stiff with rage and resentment, Cord unslung his backpack that held GUIDE and half-flung it at Lathan. The man caught it neatly, one-handed, and gave Samella another of his cool smiles.

"Like I said, very perceptive," he said. "I hope you can also keep these hot-headed kids from coming after me."

Samella ignored the remark, her gaze unflinching. "If that's not your ship out there," she asked, "whose is it?"

"That's what I'm going to find out," Lathan replied. "But it probably belongs to some . . . acquaintances of mine. And if I were you, I'd stay away from them. They're even less friendly than I am."

"They must be a lotta fun," Jeko muttered.

"In fact," Lathan went on, "my advice to you kids is to go a long way from here. These badlands can be unhealthy for you, for many reasons."

He looked at them silently for a moment, with that tinge of sadness, or sympathy, once again briefly visible in his cool gaze. Then he wheeled and sprang up the slope, with the swift litheness of an athlete, and vanished from sight among a cluster of rocks.

4

Cave of Mystery

The teenagers stood where they were, staring up at the slope where Bren Lathan had disappeared.

"What now?" Samella asked quietly. "Do we go somewhere more peaceful, like he said?"

Cord looked at her sharply, then saw that she was smiling her wry, crooked smile. "Maybe we should," he said sourly. "But I want to go after him."

"What else?" Heleth demanded. "The yeck-head stole GUIDE."

"I'd like to run inta him without his gun," Jeko snarled.

"And we oughta have a look at whoever's on that ship," Rontal added.

Samella, still smiling, nodded when Cord glanced at her, and so it was settled. "There's no point trying to track him," Cord said. "Even if we could find his trail in these rocks, he might use that gun if we get too close to him. Let's head for the spaceship, like we set out to do. We know more or less where it is, from GUIDE. And we'll probably find Lathan, too, somewhere around there."

So they clambered to the top of the slope, none of them feeling sorry about leaving the lake behind. Beyond the crest of the slope was a shallow gully, cluttered with rock and gravel. When it petered out, at the junction of two bare ridges, they had to climb another slope, where they found another stretch of lower ground on the far

31

side. So it went, for more than an hour of tiring progress over the folds and creases of that forbidding region.

Eventually they paused, to rest weary legs, to sip some water and dig into their dwindling supply of food concentrates. The others were talking in low voices, but Samella was silent, with a faraway, thoughtful expression. Cord had no doubt about what was on her mind.

"Trying to figure Lathan out?" he asked.

Samella's gaze returned to normal, and she nodded. "Except I can't. A strange man . . ."

"He'll be a lot stranger when I meet up with him," Heleth said belligerently.

"Think you can take him alone?" Jeko asked mockingly. "He comes on hard."

"Right," Samella said before Heleth could reply. "He seems like a hard man, cold and dangerous. But then he does things that a really cold-blooded man wouldn't do."

"Like saving us from the monster," Cord said.

"Or like just leaving us alive," Samella said. "And looking, once or twice, as if he was sorry for us."

"You noticed that, too," Cord said. "Seemed odd."

"Everything about him is odd," Samella went on. She raised a slim hand, ticking off the points on her fingertips. "A man lands on a wild planet—in an escape module, because he says his ship blew up. He's armed and seems able to take care of himself. When he meets us, he acts cold and harsh, yet he saves our lives. He wants to keep his presence a secret from ColSec, yet he doesn't harm us even though we know his secret. He gets upset when he hears about the other ship, takes GUIDE and rushes off. Yet he warns us about the people from the ship and looks as if he feels sorry for us. And all the while, behind his hard-man act, he seems troubled and scared and desperate. How does that all add up?"

There was a pause, while the others thought about it. To Cord, there was something strangely familiar about Lathan's situation, as Samella had described it. But it was only the nagging edge of a thought, which he couldn't work out clearly . . .

"Maybe he's actin' funny 'cause he's been stuck on Klydor," Rontal suggested. "And maybe he got excited about the ship 'cause it's a way off the planet for him."

"Could be," Samella said with a small frown. "But then why the secrecy? He's a famous space explorer—why should he worry if we know he's here?"

The answer sprang into Cord's mind at that moment, as if a door had been flung open. It was an answer born of his own grim experience in the harsh and dangerous wilderness of the Highlands. "I think I know," he said. "With him being scared and desperate, and all the secrets and hiding—he acts like someone who is being *hunted*."

"That's it," Samella said, her eyes bright. "And the people in the spaceship could be the hunters. Maybe they even had something to do with wrecking his ship—and now they've followed him here!"

There was another pause, as the others digested that thought. Then Heleth snorted, her eyes fierce. "Who cares? He's being hunted by us now, too."

"No," Cord said quickly. "We know that spaceship has to be a ColSec ship. If ColSec is hunting Lathan, then we're on his side."

"If we *take* sides," Samella said pointedly. "Maybe we should stay out of it, till we know what's going on."

Cord shrugged, seeing the sense in what she said. "Maybe. So let's start finding out."

Pulling on their backpacks, they set off again, towards another bare and crumbling slope. "Tell you one thing," Jeko said as they started to climb. "Feels funny, with all these folk on Klydor. Just when I was gettin' used to havin' nothin' but aliens and monsters and things."

33

"We'll probably run into more of those, too," Samella told him wryly, "before we're done."

Her remark turned out to be truer than any of them might have expected. As they moved on, they found that the badlands were more populated with life-forms than the gentler area that they had passed through earlier. They saw a variety of large insects, misshapen and multi-legged. They saw small crawling things with yellow shells and pincerlike claws, and slithering things whose bodies coiled and uncoiled like living springs. But the only large creatures they saw, with shaggy sloping bodies on long forelegs and short stumpy hind legs, merely roared briefly and then fled at a clumsy gallop.

While none of the creatures looked particularly dangerous, the group moved with extra care and watchfulness. Cord was still troubled by the broken and crumpled land, and all the hiding places it offered to stealthy watchers—or attackers. He no longer had the eerie sensation of being watched, but he did not entirely trust that feeling, on its own, to be an adequate warning system.

So he became even more uneasy when they reached a place that seemed to contain nothing but hiding places—in the form of caves.

Their route had brought them into an area criss-crossed with a tangle of connecting ravines. And the steep sides of the ravines were riddled with caves—high and narrow, low and flat, round and wide. They looked to Cord like an array of dark mouths, gaping as if ominously hungry. And that uncomfortable image was strengthened by the occasional cluster of sharp-edged rocks, gathered in the opening of a cave like broken and uneven teeth.

But Heleth viewed the dark openings with the purest delight. "Caves!" she breathed, her blackened face wreathed in smiles. "Now I'm getting to *like* this planet!"

She trotted ahead of the others, towards the yawning expanse of an especially large cave, and peered into its gloom.

34

"She goes in there," Jeko said with a laugh, "we'll never get her out."

Cord did not smile, for there was a grim truth behind the joke. They had no way of knowing what kind of danger might lurk within a cave in the Klydor badlands.

"Heleth . . ." he called warningly, as he and the others began to follow.

Heleth turned with a reassuring gesture. "It's empty," she said. "Nothing to worry about."

Then she stepped across the threshold, disappearing into the darkness.

Cord and the others covered the last few metres at a run. But when they drew up at the cave-mouth, they relaxed. The opening was broad enough to admit some light into the interior, and they saw Heleth standing unharmed, gazing blissfully around.

"Look!" she said. "High ceiling, dry walls, and the floor's fairly smooth, with sand on it. We could *live* in a place like this!"

"Home, sweet home," Jeko muttered.

Heleth ignored him, waving her hand at the rear of the cave. Squinting, Cord could make out patches of a deeper darkness back there—though he knew that it would seem brightly lit to Heleth. Like all of the young people she had grown up with, in the Bunkers, she had an ability to see in the dark that was wholly uncanny.

"Look at that!" she was continuing. "Tunnels—opening out of this cave. It's like a real house . . . we could have separate rooms!"

"And a monster for a roommate," Jeko said in another sour mutter.

The other four stepped farther inside the broad cave. It was dry enough, as Heleth said. But it was also chilly and dank, and the air was heavy with the mustiness of old, cold stone.

Cord and Samella exchanged glances. They both knew that a time would come, if they survived and were left alone, when they would have to choose a place on Klydor to make some kind of home. And they were both realizing that, when that time came, Heleth would want them to choose something like this cave. She would fight for her idea with all the stubborn aggression that was in her nature.

"It would make a good shelter, if the weather turns bad . . ." Cord began diplomatically.

But Heleth had caught the note of doubt in his voice, and her glare was obvious even in the dimness. "Shelter?" she spat. "This's the best place we've found on this yecky planet! It's hidden away, it's comfortable, it's solid as a . . . a bunker. What more do you want?"

She flounced furiously away towards one of the deeper patches of dimness, at the rear of the cave. Cord's eyes had adjusted slightly, and he could see that they did indeed seem to be the openings to tunnels. They were also black with an almost solid darkness, and they unnerved him.

"Heleth," he said warningly. "We don't know what kind of things live in these caves."

Heleth did not even turn around. "If there is anything," she said scornfully, "I'll see it before it sees me. And it'd probably be better company than you yeck-heads!"

And she stamped away into the forbidding blackness.

Cord moved to the rear of the cave, peering after her. How far the tunnel extended he could not tell, in the inky darkness. But Heleth had vanished entirely, and he could hear no sound.

He sighed. "We'd better go after her."

The words caused a small flicker of dismay in Samella's eyes, and Cord sympathized. Samella had been raised under the immense open skies of the prairies, just as he had been raised on the empty, wind-swept hillsides of the Highlands. Neither of them had much experience of underground tunnels—and neither was eager to gain such experience, when unknown alien creatures might lie in wait.

Rontal had seen the expression on both their faces, and he grinned. "No need for us all to go," he said easily. "Just Jeko and me. We been in a few tunnels in our time, in Limbo."

"If we get lost," Jeko said, "we'll just yell for Heleth. She'll hafta come back and get us out. I hope," he added in a low voice.

With some relief, Cord agreed. "Just be careful," he told them.

Jeko's grin was lopsided. "Fell', we been careful since we got to Klydor. Not gonna stop now."

The two Streeters loped away, into the dark passage where Heleth had entered. Cord and Samella—too edgy to settle down and wait calmly—began wandering around the dim breadth of the large outer cave, to find some distraction.

They found a little when they peered into another of the tunnel mouths, farther along the rear wall of the cave. In it they saw a faint, ghostly glow, and realized that it came from a thin, soft growth on the stone, like a lichen, with a natural phosphorescence.

"I hope this stuff grows all along the tunnel," Samella said, prodding at the growth. "Even Heleth's eyes need a *bit* of light—and this ought to be enough for her."

Cord felt some relief at that. "It's strange, how she got that way," he said, as they wandered away towards another tunnel mouth. "How they all got that way, in the Bunkers. Eyes like owls and hearing like cats."

Samella nodded. "The Bunkers have had people in them for years—generations. I suppose it's a kind of natural adaptation, like you get with some animals when their environment changes."

Cord blinked, not quite sure that he knew what she was talking about. He was beginning to ask Samella to explain further, when they reached the dark mouth of the next tunnel.

His mind went suddenly blank with shock, and he heard Samella's sharp intake of breath. Around him the shadows of the cavern seemed to gather more menacingly, as he stared at what lay just inside the opening of that tunnel.

A man.

An adult human male, lying crumpled as if he had been flung carelessly aside by some giant hand. He was wearing a uniform of metallic blue cloth, with a dark leather belt and boots. It was a uniform that Cord knew well, and hated fervently. But Cord was not looking at the man's clothes. His shocked stare was fixed on the man's face.

The features were twisted slightly, in an expression of pain. And that expression would never change, for the man was staring up with the empty sightless eyes of the dead.

5

The Hunters

"Now we know," Samella said shakily, "who arrived on that spaceship."

Cord shook himself, to drive away the feeling of icy menace gathering around him. With an effort he took his eyes from the dead, contorted face and studied the blue uniform. The last time he had seen such a uniform, he had just received an injection, and he was sliding into a coma-like sleep—from which he awoke months later, in a spaceship, hurtling towards an alien world.

It was the uniform of the Civil Defenders, the cruel and violent security force of the Organization.

"So Bren Lathan is being hunted by the CeeDees," Samella said thoughtfully. "All the way to Klydor. I wonder what he's done?"

Cord shrugged. "Nothing to do with us. I want to know what this CeeDee was doing here, in this cave."

"And what killed him," Samella added. "There's not a mark on him."

"Not that we can see," Cord said. Gritting his teeth, he stooped and heaved the corpse over on to its face. Then he straightened, staring grimly down.

The wound was clearly visible, even in the dimness. A narrow gash, in the back of the man's neck, just above the leather collar of his tunic. A stab wound.

"Did Lathan have a knife?" he asked.

"I didn't see one on him," Samella said. "Anyway, how do we know he did this?"

"Who else?" Cord said. He glanced over his shoulder. "I wish the others would get back. We've got to get out of here."

Samella seemed hardly to have heard him. She was peering intently into the black depths beyond the tunnel-mouth where the corpse lay. "Cord, there's something in there," she said.

Cord's gaze followed her pointing finger. There *was* something —just a shadow among the other shadows, on the sandy floor of the tunnel. As he squinted, trying to make it out, Samella moved forward, slipping like another shadow into the tunnel's blackness.

"Wait," Cord said anxiously. He started to follow, then hesitated, stumbling slightly, for the corpse lay directly in front of him.

"It's his helmet," Samella's voice said from the darkness. "Can you see?"

Cord saw the shadowy movement as she held up the object, and he recognized its rounded shape—and the faint sheen of blue metal.

"There's something else," Samella said, her voice almost inaudible as she moved deeper. "A little farther in."

Cord sighed and began to step around the dead CeeDee, to follow her into the blackness. But then he heard a soft scrape on the sand-covered rock behind him. Recognizing the sound as that of boots on the cave floor, he turned with relief to greet his three friends.

But the relief vanished in another stomach-clenching jolt of shock.

Standing in the brighter light at the opening of the large outer cave, he saw five men. They were staring at him with amazement, and also with something like anger. Each of them was carrying a heavy, stubby object that had to be some kind of weapon. And each of them was wearing the blue uniform of the Civil Defenders.

*

"Kid," said one of the five men, "I don't know where you came from, but I wouldn't count on you gettin' back there in one piece."

As he spoke, in a hoarse rasping voice, the man began to saunter forward across the cave floor. Cord stood still, his heart pounding, as he stared at the group. The man moving towards him was slightly shorter than the others, but they were all powerfully built, broad-shouldered and heavy-boned. Their faces were similar, too—not in the features but in the expressions. Their surprise, at the sight of Cord, had faded. The faces were set in bleak hard lines, etched with contempt and arrogance.

And the eyes were the worst. Cord had seen eyes like that only on wild, vicious predators. There was an emptiness in them—an absence of feeling, of humanity, as if these five men had lost their souls in a lifetime of cruelty and violence.

The man who had spoken was closer now, and Cord, seeing the brutal, thin-lipped face more clearly, felt his heart turn to cold stone. On that face, just below the cheekbones, were small, light-coloured tattoos, in a swirling pattern. The same markings were just visible on the faces of the other men. And they were probably on the face of the corpse, at Cord's feet, though he had not noticed them in the dimness.

The tattoos, he knew, were a special insignia. They meant that the five men were not just CeeDees. They were Crushers.

The Crushers were an elite force within the Civil Defenders. They were trained, to an incredible level of skill, in every form of combat, with weapons or unarmed. And they were used against the very worst offenders—anyone foolhardy enough to dare to oppose the rule of the Organization. At the merest whisper of resistance, at the first glimmer of rebellion, the Crushers were sent into action. And the would-be rebels were savagely, murderously, crushed.

Cord knew some of this from Samella, but some of it also from the manic killer called the Lamprey, who had been one of the survivors of the crash-landing on Klydor. The Lamprey had once been a Crusher—he had probably been too insane even for that brutal force—and had boasted of some of the monstrous things that the Crushers did to enemies of the Organization.

The part of Cord's mind that could think sensibly told him that Bren Lathan must be considered a very dangerous person, if six Crushers had come hunting him through outer space.

The shorter man had moved to within a few steps of Cord. He was still idly carrying his bulky weapon in one hand. And he had not taken his eyes from Cord's face.

"Throw the stick to one side, kid," the hoarse voice ordered, "and step back."

Cord had almost forgotten about the club in his hand. He glanced at the other four men, standing poised and watchful in the cave mouth. Wordlessly, he tossed the club on to the ground and moved backwards a step or two.

Only then did the shorter man look down at the corpse on the floor. In a moment the blank eyes swung back to Cord. "Why'd you kill him?" the man rasped.

Cord stared, struggling to find his voice. "I didn't. I don't even have a knife."

The man's expression did not change. "It'll be around here somewhere. Where you dropped it." The ugly eyes swept Cord up and down. "Let's hear something about you."

"He's a ColSec scard, Captain Warreck," snarled one of the other men. "Lookit his clothes."

"So there's a colony round here somewheres," said another man. "Maybe they've seen . . ."

"Shut it." The shorter man, Captain Warreck, did not raise his hoarse voice, but the speaker's mouth clamped shut like a trap. Warreck continued to examine Cord, as someone might study a bug under a microscope. "Start talkin', kid."

Cord's jaw set hard, as anger began to smoulder within him.

"Scard" was the contemptuous CeeDee term for young offenders who were to be exiled—discarded—on alien planets by ColSec. Cord had hated the term when he first heard it, though he had not fully known then what it meant. He hated it even more, now. Yet he tried to curb his anger, as he replied.

"My name's Cord MaKiy. And there's no colony. The ship crash-landed, and there were only a few survivors . . ."

He stopped abruptly, fearing that he might be saying too much.

"So where're the others?" Warreck demanded.

"Around . . . somewhere," Cord said. "I'm not sure. I wandered off on my own."

"Wandered in here and killed this officer," Warreck rasped. "Why?"

"I didn't," Cord said angrily.

Again Warreck looked him up and down, his expression unchanged. "We'll just have to find another way to ask you. You won't enjoy it much."

He half-turned towards his men. "Bring him. If he tries anythin', shoot his legs. Keep him alive for a while."

The others started forward. But as they moved, a burst of sound erupted like the flaming roar of a rocket. Cord jerked with shock as a ribbon of dazzling yellow energy seared through the air, only centimetres past Warreck's head.

"Stand still!" Samella's voice shouted from the darkness of the tunnel. "Or the next one takes your head off!"

Warreck had turned his back to the tunnel mouth when he had spoken to his men. He went rigid, though his face remained as impassive as before.

"Throw the gun into the middle of the cave!" Samella ordered. "Carefully!"

Warreck jerked his hand, and the heavy weapon sailed away, thudding into the sand. He did not even look at it, but stared

43

straight ahead, empty-eyed. The other men had snapped their guns up as soon as Samella had fired—but they had not used them. They could not see Samella in the tunnel, and their captain's bulk was standing between them and Cord.

"Now tell your men," Samella shouted, "to throw their guns down there, too, and to move back against the wall!"

Warreck did not turn his head, barely moved his thin lips. "Do it," he rasped.

The other four flung their weapons down, near the captain's gun, and moved back.

"Move over there with them!" Samella snapped to Warreck. "Slowly!"

Warreck stalked across the cave, stiff-backed. Then Samella stepped out of the tunnel, eyes blazing, with another of the strange guns in her hands, training it on the five glaring men.

"It's the dead man's gun," she explained in a hurried whisper, as she came to stand beside Cord. "He must have dropped it back in the tunnel." She glanced at Cord. "Any ideas?"

"I feel like Lathan must have felt with us," Cord murmured. "It'd be safer to shoot them down—but I couldn't do it."

"I wouldn't think much of you if you could," Samella replied.

"Let's get out of here," Cord said. "If they come after us, we can lose them in the rocks."

"What about Heleth and the boys?" Samella asked.

"We'll circle back later," Cord said. "We'll find them somehow."

"If these killers don't find them first," Samella said. "They're Crushers—did you see?"

Cord nodded bleakly. "We have to risk it," he said, still in a low voice inaudible to the Crushers. "If this bunch comes after us, the others can get out of the cave safely. And it'll be dark soon, so Heleth will have the advantage, even outside."

"Right," Samella agreed. "Let's go."

They began to sidle towards the cave opening, Samella keeping her gun carefully aimed at the five silent but furious men. But as they passed the other five weapons, which had been flung into the middle of the cave, Samella paused. Again the cave filled with sudden brilliance as the beam of energy erupted from her weapon. And when it stopped, the five guns on the floor lay in a shattered, molten ruin.

Then the two of them moved on. Only when they reached the brightness at the cave-mouth did they hear the rasping, ugly voice of Captain Warreck.

"We'll meet again," he said. "Gun or no gun. And you'll be a long time dyin'."

6

Tunnel of Terror

Cord shifted his shoulders restlessly against the chill stone. He and Samella were tucked into a narrow crevice, high on a steep slope, screened by a spread of brush. It offered both a hiding place and a useful view of the slopes and gullies around it. But they had been crouching there for nearly an hour, without moving, and the inactivity was beginning to irritate Cord. So were the several sharp points of rock, jabbing into his back. In fact, just then, a great many things were irritating him.

Too many mysteries and anxieties had been flung at him during that day. There was all the mystery surrounding Bren Lathan, the mystery of the dead CeeDee in the cave, the mystery of why a team of Crushers was hunting Lathan. And there was the growing worry about Heleth and the boys, not to mention a worry about the alien life-forms that might be prowling the nearby rocks, as twilight began to gather.

Cord disliked having to be still for any length of time, and he also disliked having to run and skulk and hide, even from an enemy as dangerous as five Crushers. Most of all, he disliked having a head full of puzzles and worries. His natural instinct was to *do* something—anything—about his problems.

"We must have lost them," he muttered to Samella. "Or they would have shown up by now."

He saw Samella's crooked smile and knew that she was perfectly aware of his restlessness. That fact irritated him even more. But her voice was matter-of-fact.

"Then we can relax a little," she said. "Do you want to eat something?" She reached up to the straps of her backpack.

Cord shook his head. "Maybe later. Let's head back to the cave while there's still some light."

He eased himself forward, peering around. Satisfied that no enemies were in sight, he stepped gratefully out of the crevice, Samella behind him.

"I don't think they'd try to jump us while we've got this," he said, hefting the strange gun. He had taken charge of its weight when they had scrambled up to the crevice. "They've probably gone back to their ship."

"Don't be too sure," Samella said. "They outnumber us—and they're Crushers."

"I know," Cord said sourly. "But I almost wish they *would* try something." He squinted along the gun's barrel at an inoffensive boulder. "I'm just in the mood to shoot something."

Samella smiled again. "Be careful, that's no laserifle. I read about it once—it's a new weapon, producing a bolt of raw energy. It's even self-generating—never runs out. I don't really understand how it works. But they call it a 'sun-gun'."

"We don't need to understand it," Cord said gruffly. "We just need to know how to use it."

They moved away, like shadows in the deepening dusk. When they had fled from the cave, where they had left the five disarmed Crushers, Cord and Samella had tried to stay on patches of bare rock, as much as possible, to leave no obvious trail. Now they continued that careful progress, also keeping a wary watch on the landscape around them, half-expecting at any moment to see a threatening glimpse of blue uniforms.

The cave where they had been was more than a kilometre away, and they had followed a winding, zig-zag route in their flight. But

Cord was at home in that kind of terrain and had a clear idea of where the cave lay, so they could follow a more direct route back to the cave. It was still light enough for them to see fairly well when they reached the tangle of ravines, where the multitude of caves were yawning gapes of absolute blackness.

As they crept cautiously along a ravine, the tension that gripped Cord flared into sudden fear. He had caught sight of a shadowy movement at the edge of his vision. But then he saw that it was only one of the large, slope-backed beasts that they had seen earlier—and it had vanished swiftly into a small cave.

"I hope a family of those hasn't moved into our cave," Samella whispered.

"We'll just move them out," Cord replied dourly.

In stealthy silence they approached the broad opening of the cave that they were seeking. For a long moment they paused at the entrance, peering into the darkness, listening hard. At last they were as certain as they could be that nothing was lurking within.

Cord glanced around, spotting a clump of dry brush sprouting nearby. "Let's gather some of that," he said. "For torches."

"Is that safe?" Samella asked dubiously.

"We'll light them when we get farther inside," Cord replied. "No one will see the flame unless they're right in front of the cave. And I want to look at that tunnel floor. The others might have left tracks, to show that they've come out."

"I hope they have," Samella said anxiously. "If they're still in there . . ."

She did not need to finish the sentence. Cord knew that if Heleth and the boys had not come out of the tunnel, it would be because they had run into trouble—and might never be coming out.

He shook himself, to throw off that chill thought, and went to the clump of brush, tearing away two handfuls of the dry and crackling branches. Then he and Samella crept into the black interior of the cave.

Their boots made no sound on the soft sand of the cave floor as they moved, one careful step at a time, deeper into the darkness. They could see absolutely nothing ahead of them—but also they could hear no sound. The cave was as silent, musty and dank as before.

Their groping fingers finally touched the rear wall of the cave. "Let's risk it," Cord said quietly. He turned away from Samella and fired a short burst from the sun-gun.

The yellow dazzle was almost painful, after that total darkness. But the blast had lit the bundles of brush, and the orange flicker of the makeshift torches was a reassuring sight.

In that unsteady light, they saw that the remains of the five guns, which Samella had destroyed, no longer lay on the cave floor. Also, as they had expected, the dead man was gone. So the Crushers had almost certainly headed back to their ship, carrying the corpse of their companion. And probably getting fresh weapons, Cord thought grimly.

Too many boots had churned through the sand of the floor in the large outer cave, and Cord could make no sense of the footprints. So he and Samella moved to the mouth of the tunnel that Heleth and the two Streeters had entered.

The torchlight showed that the tunnel was narrow and low, its sides and roof slabbed with bumpy, pitted rock. Farther into its depths, beyond the reach of the torches, Cord saw a vague, ghostly glimmer and remembered the patches of phosphorescent lichen. But he could see that the faint glow could never provide enough light for himself or Samella, even if it would do very well for Heleth's cat-eyes.

They took a few careful steps into the tunnel, and then Cord glanced down. The floor was made more of crumbled dirt than sand, and it took a footprint fairly well. The marks of three pairs of boots were clear to Cord, and he could even make out the differences in sizes of the three teenagers who had entered the tunnel.

But all the tracks led inwards. There were no footprints suggesting that anyone had come out.

Cord and Samella looked at each other fearfully. "We have to go in and look for them," Samella said.

Cord nodded glumly, then glanced at the bundle of brush, flaring and smoking. "We can't go too far," he said. "The torches won't last very long."

Samella stared into the tunnel's ominous blackness. "Could we try calling them?"

"When we're farther in," Cord said. "The sound won't carry far, outside the cave."

Samella nodded and they moved forward, torches held high, Cord gripping the sun-gun tensely in his other hand. A few metres farther on, they stopped again, and Cord peered down at the tunnel floor.

His eyes brightened. The dirt floor held another muddle of prints, not easy to make out. But it looked very much as if two pairs of boots—Jeko's and Rontal's, Cord thought—had been walking *out* of the tunnel, at this point. He showed Samella what he had found, and she frowned thoughtfully.

"You mean they may have come back this far," she asked him, "and then stopped?"

"Maybe they saw the Crushers," Cord suggested.

"Maybe," Samella agreed, "or heard them."

"I can't be sure," Cord said, "but it looks as if they turned around here, and went *back*, deeper into the tunnel."

"I hope they had Heleth with them," Samella said. "They'd need her, in here."

The two of them moved silently on, Cord in the lead, both of them feeling a chill that was more from anxiety about their friends

50

than from the tunnel's dankness. Cord was watching the torches carefully, knowing that they would soon have to turn back—or go on in a total, mind-numbing blindness.

"We could try giving a yell now," he said to Samella, over his shoulder.

He heard her draw breath to call the names of their friends. But he was completely unprepared for what happened next.

He heard a faint scraping sound. Suddenly Samella was staggering sideways, half-falling against the tunnel wall. And the darkness echoed and re-echoed, with her wild scream of pure agony and terror.

7

Awakening

Cord whirled, as Samella screamed again and again. The sound, amplified by the tunnel, battered at his senses, and the horror before his eyes immobilized him, as if his limbs were too heavy to move.

The screaming, writhing Samella appeared to be bound. What looked like a coil of heavy, flattish cable was wrapped around her upper body, pinning her arms to her sides. The coil glistened slightly, in the light from Cord's torch, and seemed as rough and mottled as the tunnel walls.

That moment of frozen, staring horror seemed endless, but in fact it was only a fraction of a second before Cord reacted. He dropped the gun, knowing he could not fire for fear of hitting Samella. But he kept a tight grip on the torch as he sprang forward to free the girl from the snake-like creature that had gripped her. He was snarling, with teeth bared, as his free hand clutched the thick coil, trying with all his surging strength to rip it away.

Nausea rose within him at the slippery, ice-cold feel of the creature. Its body was thicker than Cord's arm, solid and flexible muscle, and its underside held countless small indentations like suction cups, clinging with an unbreakable grip to the shrieking girl. Cord heaved with furious power, but with no effect. The coil remained clamped around Samella. And there seemed to be no end to the monster—head and tail were out of sight, as if tucked away beneath the tightening coil.

Samella, still screaming, was dragged back and forth as Cord fought with the monster. But then Cord brought his other hand into the battle—and thrust the flaring torch against the horror's slimy hide.

The flames hissed, and Cord could feel a ripple in the muscular coil, a powerful flexing as the monster tried to draw away from the fire. For an instant the ghastly pressure around Samella seemed to loosen. And, still gripping the snaky body with one hand and wielding the torch with the other, Cord exerted all his strength in one frantic heave.

Samella shrieked again as that mighty pull dragged her off her feet, tumbling her to the tunnel floor. But part of the coil had been jerked away from her body. And with it, the monster's head emerged—from where it seemed to have been buried in Samella's back.

The head was an ugly triangle, with small red glaring eyes. But Cord was looking with horror at the way that the head tapered into a long, narrow beak—a beak shaped like a blade. And on the point of the blade-beak was a dark, thick smear that was undoubtedly blood. Samella's blood.

The sight poured a wild but icy fury through Cord's powerful body. He saw, as if in slow motion, the baleful red eyes flash and the beak strike towards him, stabbing like a sword. But he seemed to have all the time he needed to change his grip, to fling up his right hand and catch the monster's neck, steely fingers sinking deep into the slippery flesh. And with his other hand he thrust the torch full into those unblinking red eyes.

The whole muscular length of the monster jerked and shuddered, as it tried to pull away. In one powerful convulsion, it swung all of its long body free of Samella and flung itself forward, to coil around Cord.

Again, Cord seemed to see the attack in slow motion. He met it with another surge of raging strength, and hurled the monster away

53

from him. The deadly coil twisted and flailed in mid-air, then smacked against the rocky wall of the tunnel.

It righted itself in an instant, slithering up the wall towards a narrow crevice, from where it must have dropped out of the darkness on to Samella. Cord swiftly reached down to the sun-gun that he had dropped and snatched it up. The yellow flame roared dazzlingly as, almost without aiming, he fired and cut the monster in two.

Then he let the gun fall again, ignoring the threshing death throes of the monster, and knelt beside Samella. She was slumped on the floor, sobbing and moaning. As Cord tried gently to lift her up, he could barely make out what she was saying.

"My back . . ."

Feverishly, still working one-handed as he held up what was left of the torch, Cord tore the backpack away from her and jerked up the back of her tunic. Raw panic clawed at his mind as he stared at the blood dripping from the wound—a narrow slit, like a knife-wound—between her shoulder-blades.

Then Samella seemed to sigh, very softly, and her body crumpled and sagged until she was a dead weight on Cord's supporting arm.

Numb with terror and despair, Cord saw at last the connection between the blade-like beak of the monster and the fatal wound on the dead CeeDee in the cave. But the realization meant nothing to him, and he was hardly aware of it. Nor was he aware that tears were blinding him and that he was shouting Samella's name, over and over.

Then through his anguish one gleam of awareness penetrated like an electric shock. He could feel a slight movement against his arm, steady and repeated.

She was still breathing.

Afterwards he would never remember the mindless reflex that made him drop the torch, now almost burnt out, and scoop up the sun-gun in his free hand. He would never remember how, lifting Samella in the circle of one arm as if she were weightless, he stumbled back along that tunnel of horror, across the large outer cave, and into the full darkness of the night.

Nor would he remember how he climbed up a bumpy slope of rock, with only the fitful light of alien stars to show him the vague shapes of rocks looming in the darkness. But he climbed until he found a narrow ledge, no more than half a metre wide. There he lowered himself, his back against the rock wall that rose above the ledge. His one arm was still around Samella, protectively, her upper body resting across his lap. And there he sat, motionless, the sun-gun gripped solidly in his hand, glaring into the night as if daring all of Klydor to come against him.

For hour upon hour, he sat as if he were carved from stone. His eyes did not waver, the muzzle of the gun did not droop. His every sense, his entire being, was focused on the alien night, except for that part of his hearing that listened tensely to the soft, continuing whisper of Samella's breathing.

But his inner vision would not let go of the sight of that oozing wound in the centre of her back. He had no idea how deep it was, or what internal damage it might have done. And he could do nothing about it. The medi-kit that had been brought from the shuttle was in Rontal's backpack. But even if he had it, Cord knew that his lack of skill, and the darkness, would have made it of little use.

All he could do was sit there, protecting the unconscious girl, fighting against the agonizing knowledge that she might be dying from that wound.

Dawn arrived at last, almost without Cord noticing. Samella had hardly moved during the hours of darkness, yet her breathing remained steady and untroubled. Cord had also not moved all that time, fiercely blocking from his mind the increasing pain of cramped joints and stiff muscles. So he was dully surprised when the dim light of early morning gave him back the full use of his eyes.

But he was startled, like being awakened by a slap in the face, when Samella gave a moaning sigh, stirred slightly, and opened her eyes to stare up at him.

"Have we been here all night?" she asked wonderingly.

Cord nodded, struggling to make his voice work. "Are you . . ." he said stumblingly. "How do you feel?"

"Stiff and sore," Samella said.

"But your back," Cord went on urgently. "I thought you were dying . . ."

He saw her eyes cloud, felt her shudder, as she relived the memory of that horror in the tunnel. But then her self-control asserted itself.

"It hurts a little," she said. "Will you look at it?"

Cord helped her to sit up, stiff muscles responding slowly. He lowered the sun-gun, discovering that the hand that had gripped it for all those hours was entirely numb. Awkwardly, he raised the back of Samella's tunic, to inspect her wound.

And joy flooded through him, sweeping away fear and anxiety as if an enormous pressure had been lifted from his shoulders.

Seen in the morning light, the stab-wound between Samella's shoulder-blades was clearly superficial. The bleeding had stopped, with dried blood crusted around the gash, and Cord could see that the ghastly blade-beak of the monster had penetrated less than a centimetre into the flesh.

"It doesn't *feel* very serious," Samella said, with a question in her voice.

"It isn't," Cord said, pulling her tunic down. "But I don't understand why . . ."

Samella looked puzzled, and it suddenly came to Cord that she had never really *seen* the horror that had wrapped itself around her. So, in as few words as possible, he described it, expecially the knifelike beak, and saw her face twist with revulsion. He felt the same sickness within himself as he recalled that frantic struggle in

56

the darkness. But then, as he thought about it, he saw the answer to the puzzle. Vividly he remembered the ghastly beaked head swaying up towards him, after first pulling back and away from . . .

"The backpack!" he said abruptly. "The thing stabbed through your backpack—so it only nicked you!"

Samella blinked, then smiled faintly. "That must be it. Maybe it hit a food container or something, on the way."

"And I was nearly sure you were dying, when I brought you up here," Cord said.

Samella looked around at the ledge where they sat, and her eyes were full of gratitude. "I suppose I passed out, and then just . . . stayed asleep. It was a long, hard day." She looked worriedly at Cord. "And you look like you haven't closed your eyes or relaxed all night."

"I haven't," Cord said simply. Then he grinned. "But I feel better now than I expected to last night. And I'll be even better when we get moving."

"Where to?" Samella asked—and the nervousness in her tone showed that she already knew the answer.

"Back to the cave," Cord said dourly. "Your backpack, with our food, is still in the tunnel. And as far as we know, so are Heleth and the boys."

Samella's hands twisted tensely in her lap. "Maybe they ran into more of . . . those creatures, in the tunnel."

"Maybe," Cord agreed bluntly. "Or maybe they're all right and waiting for us to come back. They could even be out in the open wandering around looking for us. But the only place we can start finding out is in that cave." He put a hand gently on her shoulder. "You can wait here, and I'll go."

Samella took a deep breath, fighting for the control that was so much a part of her. "No. I'll come with you."

Cord squeezed her shoulder, then rose slowly to his feet, feeling that his muscles and joints were creaking as audibly as an old gate.

Samella, too, was wincing as she stood up, but readily fell in beside him as they began to descend from the ledge.

A sudden sound almost made him lose his footing on the crumbling slope. They halted, tense and wide-eyed, listening to the echoes.

In the distance, a human voice had cried out—a wild yell that mingled anger and fear, and that had been almost instantly cut off.

8

Reunion

Cord leaped down the slope, Samella at his shoulder, and sprang away along the ravine at the bottom. All aches and stiffness were forgotten, for both were convinced that the cry had come from one of their missing friends. They ran steadily, not at a frantic sprint, and did not neglect to keep a careful watch on the landscape around them.

Despite their caution, they covered a considerable distance within the first moments after the echoes of the yell had faded. Then Cord slowed their pace. Whoever it was that had cried out, someone—or something—had cut that cry off. Cord had no wish to blunder, with Samella, into the teeth of some new menace.

"Up there," he murmured, gesturing towards a craggy promontory a few hundred metres away. "We'll take a look around."

They moved forward as quietly as they could, tense and watchful. Another series of overlapping slopes and crests led them at last to the vantage point that Cord had selected. Crouched nearly double among a cluster of gnarled outcrops of rock, they crept to the summit and looked down.

For a long moment, neither of them took a breath.

Below them, on the sandy floor of a gully, they saw three of the five CeeDee Crushers—Captain Warreck and two of his men.

Cord saw that the blue-uniformed Crushers had certainly gone back to their spaceship, for they were no longer unarmed. They had dark leather holsters strapped round their waists, and the holsters held long-barrelled hand guns, another form of Earth's high technology that Cord had never seen before.

But he spared the guns only the briefest of glances. His attention was fixed on what one of the Crushers was doing—and to whom.

Bren Lathan lay sprawled face down in the sand of the gully. His silvery jumpsuit was streaked with dirt, and a red smear of blood showed in the close-cropped hair at the back of his head. His arms were pulled behind his back, and Cord could see the glint of metal restrainers being clamped on his wrists and ankles.

The bulky figure of Captain Warreck stood over Lathan, staring impassively down. The man who was fastening the restrainers completed the task, then gathered up the crude backpack that contained GUIDE from where it had been lying beside the still figure of Lathan. The other man picked up Lathan's laserifle and handed it to Warreck. Cord saw that he muttered something, though the sound did not carry to his and Samella's hiding place. But they could hear Warreck's rasping reply.

"Got to keep him alive," Warreck said. "Lots of folk will never believe that Bren Lathan is the rebel leader, unless they see him at his trial."

The other man made some reply, and Warreck's thin lips twisted in a mockery of a smile. "Oh, yeah," he said. "After the trial, we take him apart, slow, till we get the name of every other rebel there is."

He jerked his head and turned away. The others hoisted Lathan from the ground, handling his weight with ease, and the three marched off along the gully with their prisoner.

Cord and Samella drew nervously back among the rocks. The relief that Cord had felt at seeing that the person who had cried out was not one of their missing friends had been swept away by anger and outrage. Whatever he might feel about Bren Lathan, he would not wish him or anyone to fall victim to the Crushers. Especially not if Lathan really was what Warreck had said . . .

"Did you hear that?" Samella said. "Lathan is the leader of some kind of *rebellion*!"

"Not any more, he's not," Cord said bleakly.

Samella swung to face him, eyes bright with determination. "We can't just let them take him! We have to help him!"

Cord hefted the sun-gun dourly. "I wish I knew how. I suppose I could have blasted Warreck and the Crushers with him—but I was worried about where the other two might be. And all five of them have got guns again."

"I don't care," Samella said fiercely. "We have to try!"

Cord sighed. "I know how you feel. But what about Heleth and the boys? If we get shot by the Crushers we're not going to be much help to anyone."

"That's just . . ." Samella began. But Cord was never to find out what that just was. She broke off, and the two of them stiffened with new tension.

Behind them, on the slope that they had climbed, pebbles had rattled noisily down the incline—as if dislodged by something, or someone, climbing up.

Fear turned to anger and self-blame within Cord. They had let their voices grow too loud, he told himself furiously. Sound carries in strange ways among the rocks. Perhaps the two missing Crushers were creeping up the slope . . .

Gripping the sun-gun, he slid past Samella and crept forward. There was one large slab of rock jutting up like a broken portion of wall, farther down the slope. By the sound of the rattling pebbles, whoever was coming up the slope was screened from view by that slab. So they ought to be coming out from behind it, just about . . . *now* . . .

He took aim, finger poised to stab down on the sun-gun's firing stud. But instead, he did nothing—except to gape with astonishment at the fact that the gun's muzzle was aiming directly at the metal S in the forehead of Jeko, emerging from behind the rock.

Jeko's eyes went wide, then he grinned. "Don't shoot—I give up!"

"How . . . where did you come from?" Cord stammered.

"That's what we were gonna ask you," Rontal said, stepping into view behind Jeko, with a wide grin of his own.

"What about Heleth?" Samella asked, coming up beside Cord.

The grins faded from the faces of the two Streeters. "No sign of her," Rontal said glumly.

"No chance of findin' *anythin'* in that place," Jeko added. "I been in creepy places, but those tunnels . . ." He shook his head, as if unable to find words.

"Tunnels?" Samella asked quickly.

"We found out that much," Rontal said. He went on to tell them that the tunnel they had entered led to a complex network of underground passages, criss-crossed and interconnected, extending over an enormous area. And even though the two Streeters had not intended to probe too deeply into that dark and tangled maze, they had managed to get themselves lost.

"Thought we were finished," Jeko said, the shadow of remembered fear in his eyes. "Felt like bein' dead and buried. *And* blind. Just feelin' our way along, so prob'ly we took a wrong turn. We'd be wanderin' in there still, if we hadn't got lucky."

"What about . . . creatures?" Cord asked.

"Heard some snufflin' and growlin' once or twice," Rontal said. "Sounded like those big hairy things with the slopin' backs. But they kept outa our way."

"You're luckier than you know," Cord said grimly. He told them briefly about the beaked monster that had attacked Samella, and by the time he was finished Jeko's eyes were wide and staring and Rontal's face was grey.

"And Heleth is still in there," Samella said miserably.

"Could be," Rontal said. "But it's her kinda place. She can see and hear in there as good as any monster. She could just be wanderin' around, explorin', happy as anythin'."

"Not for this long," Cord said gloomily. "She'd come out to join us again."

"Maybe she started to," Jeko suggested, "and saw the CeeDees. That's what happened to us. Started comin' back, and heard voices—not yours. Then got a look at those blue uniforms." He grinned sourly. "Just like home. So we got back outa sight and went too far in. That's when we got lost—till this mornin'."

"And there's no point goin' back in lookin' for Heleth," Rontal said. "We might not get lucky again, if we got lost. If Heleth's still alive, she'll come out, sometime, and we'll find her."

Cord shook his head, feeling sick at heart at his helplessness. "We have to do something."

"Sure," Jeko said. "We head back to that cave, and we wait. That's all there is."

"And while we wait," Rontal said, "you can tell us what's goin' on. Where the CeeDees came from—where you got that gun, Cord—and why you two were up here arguin' like a coupla kids."

Cord and Samella glanced at each other, shamefacedly, and quickly explained everything that had happened since the two Streeters followed Heleth into the tunnel. When he finished, the faces of Jeko and Rontal were taut and thoughtful.

"So Lathan's runnin' a rebellion," Rontal mused.

"Then somebody oughta get him away from the Crushers," Jeko said, battle-eagerness flaring in his eyes. "Which means us."

"Cord isn't so sure of that," Samella said.

As the Streeters looked at him quizzically, Cord shook his head.

"I was thinking about you two, and Heleth," he said defensively. "And about us with only one gun, against five armed Crushers."

"Sounds like they got rippers, from what you said," Jeko put in. "The Streeters had one once. High-power guns that fire mini-grenades. Fell' gets hit with one, gets ripped to shreds."

Samella looked sick, but her voice was fierce. "It doesn't matter. We have to do *something*."

"Right," Rontal said flatly. "Cord, we got no choice. We can't go after Heleth, 'cause we'd just get lost in the tunnels again, maybe for good. And we got to go after the Crushers whether they got Lathan or not—'fore they come after us."

"Which they will," Jeko said. "You took their guns away and backed them down. That's a crime. And they'll be kinda mad about it."

Samella nodded. "We couldn't even hide from them. Their spaceship will have sensors that could spot us anywhere on the planet."

Cord did not reply at once. Empty-eyed, he stared out across the bleak ridges and ravines. It was not a natural caution, or any lack of courage, that had made him dubious about going after the Crushers. It was a feeling of foreboding, of being overtaken by calamity. Everything has gone wrong, he thought, since we came into these badlands. A few days ago, we had a world of our own, peaceful and happy and free. But now we've lost Heleth, and we have to go with one gun and two spears and fight five of the most vicious killers in the galaxy.

He took a deep breath, and stared bleakly around at the others. "I guess Rontal's right. We have no choice."

Rontal grinned and slapped him lightly on the shoulder. "We're not dead yet, fell'," he said. "If we jump them, 'stead of waitin' for them to come at us, we might get lucky. Remember, we *do* get lucky." His grin grew fierce. "And settin' Lathan loose to go on with his rebellion could hurt ColSec pretty bad."

A glint appeared in Cord's eyes, as fierce as Rontal's grin. "That's true," he said. "That would be something."

"Let's move, then," Jeko said eagerly. "And on the way, you folk with some smarts can figure out what to do when we catch up with the Crushers."

9

The Rescue

They did not have far to go. The Crushers, with their prisoner, had moved only a short distance beyond the edge of that tangled area of ravines which, as the Streeters had found, was riddled with interconnecting caves and tunnels. The blue-uniformed men had stopped in a broad, shallow basin, thick with dense patches of the dry brush that grew in the badlands. But some of the brush had been destroyed, over a wide area, so that only charred black stumps remained. And in the centre of the burnt area lay the huge, gleaming shape of the Crushers' spacecraft.

It was roughly the shape of a flattened hemisphere, and more than four times larger than the spaceship that had brought the teenagers to Klydor. The shiny hull was decorated with a huge "CD", the insignia of the Civil Defenders. And on one side of the hull, a large opening, the airlock, stood open. Near the airlock Captain Warreck and one of the Crushers lounged, stolidly eating from containers of food concentrate. Now and then there were glimpses of blue uniforms through the airlock, where the other men—or some of them—were moving around inside the ship.

Cord lay on the crest of a low cliff, overlooking the basin where the ship rested. More of the brush screened him, and the sun-gun was steady in his hands as he gazed down at the enemy—and at Bren Lathan, lying on his side near where Warreck was sitting.

Lathan appeared to be breathing, but his eyes were still closed, and he did not move. Cord wondered if the man had been hit too hard. The wound on the back of his head seemed to have stopped bleeding, but he could have a fractured skull, Cord knew, or some other internal damage.

But whatever shape Lathan was in, Cord reminded himself, it made no difference. The battle would still have to begin. The easiest thing would have been to use the sun-gun on the Crushers—but that was impossible while some of them were in the ship. So Cord and the others had worked out a plan of sorts. Samella and the Streeters were waiting, not too far away, in safety, and it was up to Cord to get things started.

I could be dead in the next few minutes, Cord thought. But the idea had no effect on him. He felt calm, emotionless. The only signs of the flow of adrenalin within him was in the clenching of his jaw and the brightness in his eyes.

Carefully, seeking to make no sound among the grey-green foliage, he eased himself forward, closer to the edge of the cliff, as if to find a clearer view.

And with that motion, and the shift of his weight, the cliff edge collapsed beneath him.

The flimsy overhang at the edge would not have been visible from where Cord lay. Countless years of erosion had carved away the cliff, leaving only a thin layer of soil—barely held together by the roots of the brush—jutting out from the top. Cord's weight, as he slid forward, had been too much for it.

He yelled as he tumbled down, a wild yell of fright that echoed from the rocks around, as a small avalanche of crumbling soil fell with him. Then he struck the ground at the foot of the cliff, a crashing thump that drove the breath from his body. The sun-gun flew from his grasp in that impact, and one leg was twisted awkwardly beneath him.

He did not try to rise. With a grimace of agony, he clutched at the ankle of the leg that had twisted under him.

"Fell down, did you, kid?" a hoarse voice rasped from behind him.

His face still contorted with pain, Cord jerked nervously around. All five Crushers were looming over him, some of them wearing ugly grins. Just as ugly were the long-barrelled guns—the rippers—that were trained on him.

He said nothing, but watched warily as the Crusher captain stooped and picked up the sun-gun from where it had fallen.

"Thought you'd sneak up and take a shot at us?" Warreck snarled.

"He coulda done it, too," one of the others muttered.

Warreck wheeled, glowering. "Nobody thought this kid would have the guts. We *all* figured he and the girl would still be runnin', fast as they could."

The other man subsided, nodding carefully, as Warreck turned his glower back on Cord. "And where's your girl-friend now? She goin' to come bustin' out to save you again?"

"Not without a gun, she ain't," another man snickered.

Cord said nothing. He tried to return Warreck's glower with a glare of his own, despite his grimace of pain. Warreck snorted and turned away, and two of the others hoisted Cord roughly to his feet.

"My ankle!" Cord cried, as his leg collapsed beneath him.

"Hurts, does it?" one of the Crushers said. He glanced down at the ankle, where the leather of the boot was taut over the obvious swelling, and his grin was vicious. "Prob'ly bust. But you'll hurt worse'n that 'fore this day's over."

They half-dragged Cord back towards the spaceship, near the open airlock, where Bren Lathan lay silent and unmoving, eyes closed, restrainers tight on his wrists and ankles. Once again Warreck confronted Cord, as the two Crushers dumped him unceremoniously on the sand.

"Let's try again," the hoarse voice snarled. "Where's the girl?"

Again Cord said nothing, glaring up from where he sat, half-slumped, within the circle of enemies.

Despite the thickness of his body, Warreck moved like a striking snake. Cord barely saw the heavy boot that flashed towards him, slamming with crushing force into his midriff. The brutal kick flung him backwards, sprawling in a flurry of sand. Moaning, clutching his middle, he dragged himself back up to a sitting position, as Warreck stepped towards him.

"*Where is she?*" he rasped.

Cord looked away, his shoulders slumping. "I don't know," he mumbled.

The captain gestured to one of his men. "Put your weight on his bad ankle a minute," he growled.

The man grinned and moved forward. But Cord scrabbled away, through the sand, one had held up feebly to ward off the attack.

"*No!*" he cried. "Don't! She's . . ." His voice cracked for an instant. "She's back at the cave," he went on in a mumble. "The same cave. With . . ."

His lips closed abruptly, and he glanced fearfully up at Warreck. But the captain had not missed that final unguarded word.

"With what?" Warreck demanded. "With who? C'mon, kid—or you'll get every bone busted to go with your ankle!"

Cord sagged miserably. "There are two others with her."

Warreck's chuckle grated, like metal on metal. "That girl shoulda come after us herself, 'stead of you," he rasped. "*She* mighta got one of us." His gaze swung to his men. "Go pick them up."

"All of us?" one of the men asked.

"All of you!" Warreck rasped. "I want them alive, so no shootin'." He gestured with the sun-gun that Cord had dropped. "I'm not gonna get any trouble from a scared kid with a busted leg, and a blank-head in restrainers with a busted skull. Get goin'!"

The four others thrust the ripper-guns into their holsters and sprang away. In seconds they were lost to view in the surrounding brush. Cord cautiously surveyed the area near the ship's airlock, spotting Bren Lathan's laserifle lying on the ground a few metres away. But it might as well have been a few kilometres away, with Warreck standing there, sun-gun in hand.

"While we're waitin'," Warreck snarled, "you can tell me a few more things. Like why you killed my officer, in the cave."

"I told you I didn't," Cord said. "There are monsters in those tunnels. Beaks like knives. That's . . ."

"Don't jerk me, kid!" Warreck rasped. He took a step forward, reaching down to grip Cord's tunic, to drag him to his feet. But as he began to pull Cord upwards, he suddenly lost his balance.

Cord had not resisted the pull. He had gone with it—surging smoothly up on to his feet as if there was nothing at all wrong with his ankle. And as he rose, he swung a fist like granite in a crashing blow at Warreck's jaw.

It was one of the hardest punches Cord had ever thrown, and it might have felled a good-sized pony. But the Crusher's trained reflexes responded. He jerked his head back, rolling it with the impact of the punch, to lessen its effect. Even so, Warreck was flung back, stumbling and half-falling, nearly on top of the still form of Lathan. But the blow had not been damaging enough.

Warreck's thin lips peeled back in a brutal snarl as he swung the sun-gun up. Cord, too, was snarling with pure fury as he tensed himself against the murderous blast of energy.

But there was no flare of yellow brightness. Instead, Cord saw a silvery blur as Bren Lathan suddenly swung his bound legs in a scything arc and swept Warreck's feet from under him.

Cord's mind went blank with surprise, but his body reacted by instinct. He leaped instantly at the fallen Crusher. And this time, off-balance and startled, Warreck had no defences against the fist that smashed into his face with furious power.

Warreck's heavy body sagged, and Cord rose slowly, holding the sun-gun, shaking his other hand where his knuckles had bruised themselves against bone. As he did so, there was a rattle of sand to the side—and Jeko and Rontal leaped into view, spears poised, with Samella behind them.

"You took your time," Cord said sourly.

"Moved as quick as we could," Jeko said, sounding aggrieved. His glance shifted to Bren Lathan, who was sitting up looking at them, as coolly as ever. "Thought you were dead or somethin'."

"So did the Crushers," Lathan said dryly. "That was the idea."

"I'm glad you weren't," Cord said. "Thanks."

Lathan nodded without changing expression, then jerked his chin at the sprawled form of Warreck. "The captain will have the key to these restrainers."

Rontal rummaged in the unconscious Crusher's pockets, and in a moment Lathan's wrists and ankles were free. Meanwhile Jeko had plucked the ripper-gun from Warreck's holster and was waving it jubilantly.

"Really worked, right?" he cried. "What a time! That fall was great, Cord—figured it was real, myself! And you looked real scared!"

"It was Samella's idea for the ankle that really worked," Cord said. He bent to unfasten his boot and tugged out a strip of cloth—a sleeve cut from a spare tunic, which he had wrapped around his ankle beforehand to make it look swollen.

"A pretty good trick," Lathan said sardonically. "Only about thirty things that might have gone wrong and got you killed."

"But they didn't, and you're free," Jeko said sharply.

Lathan inclined his head. "That's right. I don't know why you ran the risk, but I thank you."

"It makes us even," Samella said, "after what you did for us at the lake."

Lathan nodded, studying the four of them intently. Then he frowned. "Where's the other girl? With the black face?"

71

"In the caves somewhere," Rontal said. "We'll be goin' to look for her when this is over."

"But right now," Cord said, glancing around at the brush-covered basin, "we'd better move before the other Crushers come back."

Lathan raised his eyebrows. "You're not hoping that we can hide from them, are you?"

"We're not that stupid," Samella said sharply. "But we're also not stupid enough to wait for them out here in the open."

"Sorry," Lathan said wryly. "Let's go, then, and find some cover." He glanced keenly at Cord and the sun-gun. "What are you going to do? Burn them down, from ambush?"

Cord shrugged uneasily. "It sounds pretty cold-blooded. But I guess that's how it has to be . . ."

"It's the only way," Lathan said grimly. "You don't give armed Crushers an even chance." He studied Cord for a moment longer. "Why don't you let me have the sun-gun?" he said at last. "Fighting the Organization has cooled my blood a good deal."

He stepped forward, reaching out a hand in a silent request, and Cord—with some feeling of relief—handed him the sun-gun. The others were watching intently as Lathan took the weapon. In that moment, they all had their backs to the Crusher captain.

Without warning, Warreck exploded into movement.

He seemed to leap straight up from the ground, in an athletic burst of power. Lathan swung round with the sun-gun, but for an instant his aim was blocked by Cord, standing too close to him. Jeko began to whirl with the ripper-gun, but for the same instant Samella was in his way.

Moving in a blur of speed, Warreck snatched up the laserifle—lying, forgotten, nearby—and plunged into the brush at the side of the open area.

Lathan finally managed to get a shot off, and the flaring yellow beam slashed through the brush in a burst of flame and smoke. Not a sound, not a hint of movement, followed that scorching blast.

"I don't think I hit him!" Lathan snapped. "Get to cover, fast!"

The five of them turned and sprinted towards the nearest cluster of rocks. As they ran, the bright pencil-line of a laser beam seared through the air past Jeko's shoulder. The boy yelped, crouching and accelerating at the same time. Then all five of them were diving headlong behind the rocks, as another laser beam dug a deep gouge in the dark stone.

In the next instant, another part of their rocky protection trembled under the flat crash of an explosion that showered them with fragments of stone.

"Ripper!" Jeko breathed.

And Cord raised his head from the shield of rock just enough to glimpse four blue-uniformed figures, filtering carefully through the brush a few hundred metres away.

10

Deadly Pursuit

Beside him, Cord heard the flaring burst of the sun-gun, wielded by Lathan, and with it the near-silent spitting of the ripper-gun in Jeko's hand. Again lifting a cautious eye over the edge of rock, he saw the blue figures—Warreck's men, returning—crouch and vanish in the brush.

"Missed them," Jeko said angrily.

Cord lowered his head—just in time. The compact explosion of a mini-grenade sounded again on the far side of the rock where they hid. And Cord caught a chilling glimpse of the laser's vicious beam as it sliced through the air where his head had been.

"At least *we've* got the sun-gun," he said fiercely, "not them."

"Could do with a few more," Rontal growled.

The tall Streeter was glowering at the useless spear that he still held. Cord shared the feeling. He was empty-handed—since it was Samella who had thought to pick up Jeko's spear, when the boy had taken Warreck's ripper-gun. Cord found himself irrationally wishing that he still had his club, which he had left in the cave the day before.

"We'd better pull back," Lathan said, "before we get caught in a cross-fire."

He led the way, creeping along nearly on his belly, and the others followed suit. More shards of rock, hurled by exploding mini-grenades, splattered around them as they made their way among

74

the jumble of boulders and slabs. Then they halted, at the foot of a steep slope leading up to the crest of another ridge.

Lathan stared up at the slope, then pointed. "Up that way," he said. "But we'll have to move fast."

Cord followed his pointing finger, and his heart sank. Near the top of the slope, they would have to dash across an almost bare stretch of ground, fully exposed to the Crushers' guns, with gravelly soil underfoot that could prove treacherous. Cord looked around, hoping for something better. And his eyes brightened as he saw another possible route.

A long, almost vertical gash in the face of the slope reached up to the crest. It might be a cleft, what a Highland mountaineer would call a "chimney", cut deeply into the rock. It would protect them from gunfire except from someone standing directly in front of it—who would then be exposed to the sun-gun.

"No," Cord said urgently, grasping Lathan's arm. "That's a better way."

Lathan looked, narrowing his eyes, then nodded, realizing that the vertical line might well be a sizeable opening. "Right," he said. "You've got a good eye for terrain, kid."

"He's a Highland wild man," Jeko volunteered brightly. "Knows about places like this."

"And the name," Cord said tightly, "is Cord MaKiy."

The lines of Lathan's face eased as he grinned, an easy, amused grin. "Sorry," he said. "I'm never good at names when people are shooting at me. Lead the way—*Cord*."

And the Crushers would have been astonished to see that they were all grinning, as they crept away towards the cleft that Cord had spotted.

It proved to be exactly what he hoped. They could squeeze into the cleft and scramble up its rugged sides without difficulty. Cord and Lathan went first, and then the others followed while Lathan covered them with the sun-gun from above. A moment later, they were dashing down the other side of the ridge and sprinting away into the tangle of ravines and gullies.

After several twists and turns and breathless scrambling up and down more ridges, they paused for a moment's rest behind another solid fortification of rock. There they held their breaths and listened hard, but heard no sound of pursuit. Yet even then, they knew enough about the pursuers' skill not to relax completely.

"Lotsa fun," Jeko said sarcastically. "We're gonna get chased all over Klydor."

Lathan shook his head grimly. "We wouldn't last long. They've got supplies, spare grenades for the rippers—they could even lift their ship up and blast us from the air." He stared out over the bleak landscape. "They aren't going to give up and go away. And I don't really want them to. They know who I am, and they could use that to get a line on all my friends in the resistance."

"I've wanted to ask you about that," Samella broke in. "The rebellion . . ."

"If we survive, I'll tell you all about it—Samella, isn't it?" Lathan replied.

As Samella nodded, Cord interrupted. "You don't think we *will* survive, do you?"

Lathan shrugged. "I couldn't say. I'm getting the idea that I underestimated you kids—sorry, you *people*. But we have five trained and deadly killers after us. The odds are against us."

"If you're thinkin' of givin' up," Rontal said, "forget it. This fight is on, win or lose."

Lathan grinned his easy grin again. "I know. But all we can do now is keep running and hope we can find something that we can use to even out the odds a little." Again he stared around at the land. "We do have two things going for us. We have the sun-gun, and we know more about Klydor than they do. They haven't been here long enough."

"You haven't been here long yourself," Samella pointed out.

Lathan smiled at her. "I *discovered* this planet, for ColSec. I made the usual full study of it—landscape, life forms, everything."

"You'll know it better than we do, then," Cord said. "But how does that help us?"

"I don't know, yet," Lathan said. "So let's just concentrate on staying alive, in case something turns up."

A sharp hiss from Jeko startled them. "Somethin' just turned up," he said quietly, pointing.

Tension gripped them again. A quarter of a kilometre away, a blue-uniformed man stood openly among the rocks, staring in their direction. The man's size, and the laserifle in his hand, showed that it was Warreck.

Lathan began to raise the sun-gun. But Warreck swept a hand through the air, in a gesture to his unseen men, and then simply vanished among the rocks as if the ground had swallowed him.

They're good, Cord thought bleakly. They could probably teach the Highlanders a few things about moving in rough country. They're also highly trained and experienced in combat. Like Lathan says, we don't have much chance . . .

But then, trying to shake off the cold feeling of hopelessness, he turned to join the others as they stole away through the ravines.

The deadly game of hide and seek went on for more than two hours. Most of the time, the four teenagers and Lathan had no further sight of the Crushers. But they had several frightening reminders that the hunters remained on their trail. A laser beam, searing past them as they dodged behind a boulder. A mini-grenade, showering them with rock chips as they leaped up a slope.

And, even worse, another grenade exploding almost at Lathan's feet as they fled along a winding gully. But that attack had come from in *front* of them.

They swung to one side, frantically hurling themselves up the side of the gully towards the shelter of another cluster of rocks. Huddling there, they scanned the terrain around them, seeing no movement. But each of them felt sure that the Crushers were stealthily filtering towards them, invisible and relentless.

"They've spread out, circled around us," Lathan said quietly.

"So we break through," Rontal said. "Try to get *one* of them, anyway, 'fore they get us. This way, we're fish in a net."

"Or we could try something else," Lathan replied. "We could take a route where they couldn't encircle us. And where they'd be at a bit more of a disadvantage than out here."

Cord's skin crawled. He had seen Lathan's blue eyes shift sideways and upwards—to where the empty blackness of another cave-mouth gaped wide.

Samella had also followed Lathan's gaze, and her face went grey-white. "I . . . I don't think I could," she whispered.

"She was attacked in a tunnel last night," Cord explained.

Lathan raised his eyebrows. "Snaky monster, with a beak like a knife?" At Cord's nod, the eyebrows rose higher. "They don't miss. You should be dead."

"I nearly was," Samella said. Briefly, shakily, she described how the backpack, and Cord's struggles, had saved her life.

Lathan looked amazed. "Maybe we've got *three* things going for us. You people seem to be real survivors."

"We didn't get that way," Rontal said impatiently, "sittin' around waitin' for five Crushers to close in on us. Samella, the man's right—we got to do it. The tunnels will be as dark for the Crushers as for us. And they'll hafta stay bunched up together."

"That's half true," Lathan said evenly. "They'll have to stay together, but they won't be blind. They'll have lights of some sort, as part of their regulation equipment."

There was a silence as they all digested that. "No matter," Cord said dourly at last. "We'll be able to see them coming more easily."

"And maybe the snake-monsters'll get *them*," Jeko added with a savage grin.

"Not likely," Lathan told him. "Those creatures prey on other beasts, the big shaggy things with sloping backs. And the shaggy things live in the caves at *night*. So the snake-monsters hunt only at night. By day, they're dormant—harmless."

"And it's daytime," Rontal said. "So let's go."

Samella took a deep breath, straightened her back, set her lips firmly. "All right," she said.

Lathan nodded at her with approval, then slid away towards the cave, the others following.

"What we need," Rontal muttered to Jeko, "is Heleth. And a dozen more like her."

"Right," Jeko agreed. "But what we *got* is a way to get buried 'fore we get killed."

At the mouth of the cave, they paused, waiting in silence as Lathan stepped through the dark opening, sun-gun ready. Cord glanced at Samella, seeing that her eyes were huge but blank and expressionless, as if she had pulled down mental shutters behind them. For a moment her slim body trembled, in an involuntary shudder, but at once she mastered it and stood rigidly still.

Cord watched her, from the corner of his eye, with admiration and sympathy. He felt close to shuddering himself, remembering the horror in the other tunnel, the night before. And this cave looked even less appealing. The opening was narrow and high, a crude near-rectangle formed from heavy slabs of rock, like thick lips. Where other cave-mouths had seemed to be gaping in a huge yawn, this one seemed to be stretched into a scream.

Lathan stepped back out of the darkness. "Can't hear anything in there," he said quietly. "But we'll go in slow and easy." He glanced at Samella's pale, expressionless face. "And remember—those snake-things are dormant during the day."

"Hope none of them's havin' any trouble sleepin'," Jeko muttered.

Lathan smiled tightly. "I'll lead," he said, patting the sun-gun.

"Now and then I'll fire a short burst, ahead, so we can get a quick look at what the tunnel looks like. Keep close together . . ."

"We know what to do," Cord said tensely. "Let's get on with it."

Lathan nodded and stepped back into the cave, the two Streeters behind him. For a moment Samella did not move. Then, without turning her head, she stretched out a hand towards Cord. When he took it, the slim fingers were ice-cold and clutched his hand with startling strength. But then Samella looked at him and, amazingly, her mouth lifted in a hesitant smile.

Wordlessly, hand in hand, the two of them moved forward into the blinding alien darkness.

11

The Labyrinth

The silent blackness enveloped them, like a heavy, stifling cloud. With the total loss of vision, panic clawed at the edges of Cord's mind. All of his senses seemed affected—the faint scuff of boots on the uneven floor of the cave sounded impossibly remote, the dank musty air held an unreal taint of sourness. There seemed to be a metal band clamped round his chest so that he could breathe only in shallow, desperate gasps. And he could feel the enormous weight of rock and earth pressing down upon him from the roof of the tunnel, could feel the invisible walls leaning towards him as if to trap and crush him . . .

But then he became aware of a sharp pain in his hand, as Samella's fingers clenched upon his like steel pincers. The pain, and the awareness of human contact, helped him to thrust the panic away, to take the deep, shuddering breath that he had longed to take, to regain a true awareness of himself and where he was. He felt a stab of shame, as he reminded himself how much more terrible Samella's battle against panic and claustrophobia had to be.

His whisper sounded remote to his own ears. "We're all right," he told Samella, hardly aware of what he was saying. "We're together. It's all right."

Slowly, the frantic pressure of Samella's grip eased. But the two of them retained the clasp, as the group moved on.

They moved slowly in the blanketing darkness, trying not to stumble when the uneven floor thrust bumps or hollows beneath their feet. Several times they passed small patches of the strange, dimly glowing lichen. It was not enough light for Cord to see his own hand in front of him, but he glimpsed a faint shadow as one of the others, ahead, passed directly in front of the patch. That proof that his sense of sight was actually still working made Cord feel even better—and Samella's grip on his hand relaxed a little more.

Then both of them jumped uncontrollably as, with a roar, the tunnel was filled with unexpected beauty. Lathan had fired the sun-gun, and the beauty was simply a burst of golden light. For a blissful quarter of a second, they could see.

The darkness closed around them again at once, but the image of what he had seen remained vivid in Cord's mind. The walls and roof of the tunnel were cracked and seamed, pitted with niches and crevices, craggy with jutting knobs and edges of rock. The bumpy floor was hard and stony, scattered with patches of thin sand or dusty earth. It was one of the most unappealing sights that had ever met Cord's eyes.

Again they moved forward in the unrelenting darkness. But now they moved with more confidence, knowing what their surroundings looked like. And Samella seemed to be even calmer, since she and Cord had seen, in that brief flash of light, that the other three were only a stride or two ahead, looking—with sun-gun and ripper and spear—grimly able to deal with just about any danger they might meet.

After several minutes more of nearly silent progress through the tunnel, Cord heard a faint metallic clank and a murmur of warning from the blackness ahead. He and Samella halted, bracing themselves, but even so they jumped again as the sun-gun's yellow beam blazed.

In that new, short-lived burst of light, Cord saw that the tunnel was branching. The metallic clank had sounded when Lathan, in the lead, had walked with sun-gun in hand into the barrier of rock that separated the two branches.

"Maybe the Crushers'll go a different way," Rontal muttered.

"Not if they have lights," Cord said. "They'll spot our tracks."

"Probably," Lathan agreed calmly. "We can only keep going. All these tunnels are interlinked, so they might have trouble catching up with us."

They moved on, taking the right-hand branch. Two or three minutes later, Lathan again fired the gun, and they saw that the surroundings seemed little different from before. But some of the crevices and crannies in the tunnel walls seemed unusually large, Cord thought. And then he realized what they were, in the same moment as Lathan's whisper reached him.

"Secondary tunnels," he said. "We're into the depths of the tunnel network now."

"Why not duck into one of them," Jeko suggested, "and ambush the Crushers?"

"It'd be risky," Lathan replied, "if they have lights. We'd probably only get one or two of them and be cut down by the others. Better keep our distance for a while yet."

"We could use the sun-gun," Samella said, her voice sounding strained but even, "to bring part of the roof down—to block the tunnel behind us, so they couldn't follow us."

"Too dangerous," Lathan said. "I'm not sure how stable these tunnels are. We could bring the whole roof down—not just behind us but on *top* of us."

"That's a relaxin' thing to think about as we go along," Jeko muttered. "Crushers, and snake-monsters, and the roof fallin' in. Cosy."

But no one laughed as they began again to move forward in the blackness. And Cord was sure that the others would be just as chilled by Lathan's words as he was. He had been trying not to think about the scarred and corrugated roof of the tunnel, with gnarled lumps and corners of rock thrusting out as if threatening to crumble at any moment, burying them all. And the renewed tightening of Samella's hand in his showed that the same nightmare vision was appearing in her mind.

Then Lathan murmured again, and again they all halted. Cord and Samella braced themselves against the shock of the sun-gun's flame—but Lathan did not fire. And the sound that came to Cord's ears did not make him start. It made him freeze.

The sound seemed close behind them, though distorted by the echoes and amplifications of the tunnel. Yet there was no question what it was. They had heard the searing hiss of a laser beam.

The Crushers were in the tunnels, on their trail.

The sound of the laser had created such tension within Cord that he barely moved a muscle as Lathan's sun-gun flared. And this time no one used the instant of light to study the tunnel ahead. All of them had whirled, to peer back the way they had come, half-fearing that the sun-gun's light would reflect off metallic blue uniforms.

But the tunnel behind them, as far as they could see, was empty.

"They're some way away still," Lathan said softly. "Probably shooting at shadows—taking no chances."

"They'll be shootin' at us soon enough," Jeko said edgily.

"So we need to speed up," Lathan said. "I'll fire the sun-gun more often. Cord, when I fire, keep a look-out behind us."

"Fine," Cord said, trying to sound calm. But the chill was still upon him, and he could feel the slipperiness of sweat—most of it his own, he was sure—in his and Samella's handclasp.

The tension did not ease as they pressed on, stumbling more often now as they tried to increase their pace. At more frequent intervals the blast of the sun-gun filled the tunnel with yellow dazzle, and Cord's heartbeat would accelerate as he looked back. But each time there was only the forbidding rock, and the near-solid darkness.

84

After the blaze of yellow light had vanished, the group would stand still for a second, holding their breaths, and listen. Again, once or twice, they heard the ominous, distant hiss of the laser. It sounded like the Crushers had come no closer. But Cord doubted whether the distance could be guessed with any accuracy, in the echoing confines of the tunnels.

He was beginning to feel a blank fatalism, a gloomy feeling that they ought to do what Jeko had suggested earlier—find a place to ambush the Crushers and get it over with. But then he would become vividly aware, again, of Samella's slim hand in his. And though, alone, he might have halted to make a suicidal stand, putting an end to the tension and suspense, he knew that he could not do so if it meant that Samella would face the killers too.

The longer they kept going, the longer she would stay alive. It was not much, but it seemed to be the only positive thought he had. So he stumbled onwards, his mind filled with numbing nightmares, fear knotting in his stomach. Enmeshed in his own misery, he plodded forward like a robot, though dutifully turning to look back at the empty tunnel each time the sun-gun flamed. He lost track of how many times they had paused for that flash of light. He noted without interest the greater number of sizeable branching tunnels opening on either side. He had no idea how much time had passed, when Lathan finally halted them again, urging them to silence.

But then, automatically listening to the darkness, he became aware of something that had been nagging at his numbed mind for some time. And as he realized it, Lathan put it into words.

"Haven't heard that laser for a while," he whispered.

"Right," Rontal replied in the same tone. "So they could be anywhere. Wanderin' off the wrong way—or up ahead of us."

Jeko's soft laugh was mirthless. "We could all wander round here forever, lookin' for each other. Or till the monsters wake up."

"But if we could hear the laser," Samella pointed out, "they must have heard the sun-gun."

"Of course," Lathan said calmly. "That was the price we had to pay, for light."

Cord's scalp crawled. That must be it, he thought. The Crushers had heard the sun-gun and had stopped betraying their own position by firing the laserifle. So the enemy was now advancing in silence—and could be within shooting distance at any moment.

He was on the verge of demanding that they find a place to make their final stand. But the words never reached his lips.

Without warning, without the faintest sound of movement from the inky blackness around them, something had reached out. Something icy cold, something covered with a sheen of clammy wetness, something that wrapped itself in a steely encircling clasp around Cord's right wrist.

12

Creature of Darkness

The shock and terror that flashed through every part of Cord's being seemed to squeeze his throat in a grip that was as strong as the ghastly clasp around his wrist. So the wild yell that rose up within him came out as only a strangled grunt. But in the same instant he automatically and frantically jerked away, dropping Samella's hand and crashing heavily into her, flailing his muscular right arm, with all the desperate strength he could muster, to shake off the horror that had wrapped around it.

He heard a sliding scuffle in the darkness, as the threshing of his arm dragged a heavy, unseen body to one side. Then the clammy grip on his wrist fell away, and he heard a muffled thump as something struck the tunnel wall.

It had all happened in a fraction of an instant. Samella had gasped when Cord had stumbled back against her, but neither she nor the others had time to realize what had happened. So the first sound, after the solid thump on the rocky wall, was a sound that Cord had never expected to hear again.

"Ease off, yeck-head! It's me!"

The words had come out of the darkness where Cord had heard the thump, and they stunned him into silence. But Samella and the Streeters responded together, almost in shrieks of astonishment and delight.

"*Heleth!*"

Then at last Lathan fired the sun-gun, and they saw her—standing against the wall, wearing a typical Heleth scowl as she rubbed the shoulder that had slammed against the rock when Cord had flung her aside. They also saw, in that flash of light, that she flung an arm up across her eyes.

"You shoot that thing again, fell'," she said furiously, "I'll shove it down your throat. Now I'll be as blind as the rest of you for a min'."

"Sorry—Heleth," Lathan said, with both apology and amusement in his voice.

Cord vaguely understood that Heleth's remarkable night vision would have found the blaze of yellow light positively painful. But by then Cord had also realized that the girl's startling arrival, out of that total blackness, had made them all briefly forget the danger they were in.

"Heleth," he said urgently, "keep your voice down. There are five armed Crushers in the tunnels, looking for us."

"Crushers?" Heleth repeated, sounding interested but untroubled. "There's a turn. Go quiet—don't even breathe."

"What . . ." Lathan began.

"Do like she says," Rontal growled. "She can hear an earthworm diggin'."

Silence fell around them as they stood still and held their breath. And in that moment Cord found that he was feeling much more relaxed—as if the arrival of the girl from the Bunkers had eased some of the fears and tensions of their nerve-racked journey through darkness. He also sensed, from her posture next to him, that Samella, too, had relaxed—and had not renewed their handclasp.

At last Heleth broke the silence. "Nothing," she said with satisfaction. "Wherever they are, it's some ways from here. Now—what's been going on?"

It was Samella who explained, about their encounter with the

Crushers in the other cave, the rescue of Bren Lathan, and their flight from the five armed men. At the end of the brief recital of adventure, Heleth snorted.

"I thought you had some smarts," she said. "But coming in here—tunnels're no place for folk like you, blind as you are."

"We thought we'd be able to keep out of their reach, in here," Cord explained. "And we hoped that . . . that something would turn up."

"Something has," Heleth said, with a note of superiority in her voice. "Me."

Jeko laughed. "Give her the sun-gun, and let her go fight the Crushers by herself—*ow!*"

His muffled cry had been accompanied by a meaty smack that sounded to Cord like an open palm striking a hairless head.

"Just remember, yeck-mouth," Heleth said lightly, "you can't see me, but I can see you fine."

The other teenagers laughed, tension draining from them. But Lathan's sardonic words cut across the laughter. "Do you think," he said, "we could talk about what we're going to *do* now?"

The laughter subsided, but Samella's response was immediate and spirited.

"Not just yet," she said. "Not if the Crushers aren't nearby. We've just got our friend back, when we never expected to see her again. So we're going to rest for a minute or two, and find out what Heleth has been doing for two days."

Lathan sounded taken aback. "I suppose we can spare a minute or two," he mumbled.

Cord grinned in the darkness. Samella's herself again, he thought. But by then Heleth had begun the story of her own adventures—with a surprising statement.

"What I've been doing for two days," she told them, "was looking for you folk." And at their surprised noises, she explained.

She had been delighted with the tunnels when she had first

entered them, and had gone exploring, expecting the others to wait for her. After a while, she had heard Rontal and Jeko calling her. But the trouble was that the sound had come to her through a number of the branching, secondary tunnels in that complex underground maze. It was impossible to pinpoint exactly where the echoing shouts had come from. And Heleth feared that her friends had entered the network of tunnels to look for her and had lost their way.

She had searched for some hours, finding nothing. So she started towards the cave where she had left them.

"But I heard a lot more yelling and screaming," she said. "Knew it was Samella, in real trouble—but like before, I couldn't tell exactly where it was coming from."

"I'll tell you about it in a minute," Samella said flatly.

Again Heleth had begun a frantic search through the labyrinth of tunnels. But again her search had been fruitless. More hours had passed, and she had paused, exhausted, to sleep awhile. But she resumed the search when she awoke, and after more hours of searching, she had been hugely relieved to hear their voices, and to find them all unharmed.

"You're sayin'," Jeko put in incredulously, "you just went to sleep in here? With the monsters?"

"What monsters?" Heleth asked blankly. "Those beak-heads?"

"Yes, those," Samella replied. "One of them killed a Crusher, and another nearly killed me. That's why I was screaming."

"There's a turn," Heleth said wonderingly. "Never thought they'd be dangerous. They sleep a lot, and I slept when they did. And I can hear them slithering and see their little red eyes a long ways off. One went for me, once, and I broke my spear killing the yecky thing. But they're mostly no trouble." She laughed. "Rather have them than the mega-rats we get in the Bunkers."

Even Jeko was silenced by that calm statement, and Cord felt abashed. "I thought you were one of them, Heleth," he said, "when you grabbed me. Something cold and wet, wrapping round my wrist . . ."

"Sorry," Heleth said. "There's good water here and there in the tunnels, and I'd just had a drink, so my hands were wet. Thought I'd surprise you. Didn't mean to scare you."

The others laughed, and Cord was grateful for the darkness as his face reddened. "You surprised me, right enough," he admitted.

"I think," Lathan put in dryly, "we ought to get moving before the Crushers come and surprise us all."

"Not likely," Heleth told him. "I'd hear them before they got near enough to shoot."

"I'd still feel safer," Samella said, "if we knew where they are, what they're doing."

"No problem," Heleth said easily. "You keep going, and I'll go take a look at the Crushers. Then I'll come and lead you out of here and leave them hunting for you in the dark."

"Don't take any chances . . ." Cord began.

All laughter had fled from Heleth's voice. "I been playing this game in the Bunkers since about the time I learned to walk," she said. "CeeDees used to come in looking for us. We'd follow and watch, and they'd never see a thing." She paused for an instant, remembering. "Lots of them never came out again, either."

Cord felt chilled as he tried to imagine those dark pursuits, the black-faced children with their inhuman vision and hearing, drifting like ghosts through their underground world. For a second, he almost felt sorry for the CeeDees who had tried to hunt the Bunker Vampires.

"Give me a min' to get away," Heleth was adding, "before you blast that gun off again. See you."

The soft pad of her running feet was almost inaudible. Then the blanket of total silence fell around them, and they stumbled off along the bumpy, invisible tunnel.

*

91

None of them spoke as they moved steadily on. For Cord, those moments of relaxation with Heleth faded into unreality. Once again the sense of being blind and alone, being lost forever in the warren of tunnels, descended to threaten his courage. He wondered for a moment what it would be like to be Heleth—to be able to see in this blackness, to be happily at home in a narrow, stony passage beneath an unguessable weight of crushing, suffocating stone . . .

But once again he fought against the claustrophobia, and thrust it away—forcing himself to concentrate on moving as silently as he could, despite the uneven floor and the invisible twists and curves of the tunnel. And then, after nearly half an hour more of that unsteady, groping progress, Cord heard a muffled thud, a clatter of rocks, and a low snarl from Lathan.

The sun-gun flared, and in the dazzling light Cord saw that Lathan had walked into an obstruction. In front of them lay a heap of rocky rubble, piled haphazardly more than waist-high. And the clear after-image, as the yellow light vanished, showed to Cord that the rock-pile must have been formed by a partial collapse of the tunnel roof.

The thought that this part of the tunnel was even more dangerously unstable than elsewhere made Cord twice as uneasy. He had seen that they could get round the obstruction, and he wanted to urge them on. But Lathan had different ideas.

"We might wait here awhile," he said casually. "Till Heleth catches up."

"Nice place for a little ambush," Jeko suggested.

"'Specially if they couldn't be sure which way we went," Rontal said. "There's another big tunnel branchin' from this one, a short ways back."

Cord realized that Rontal must have been half-turned, when the sun-gun flared, so that he was looking back in the direction they had come from. But Cord was more concerned, just then, with the talk of an ambush.

"Lots of people have tried to ambush Crushers," Lathan said, still off-handedly. "They didn't live to tell about it."

There was something strange about Lathan, Cord thought uneasily. That casualness sounded oddly strained and forced. What was going on in his mind? But then the thought fled, and he stiffened with tension at the soft padding sound behind them.

"Don't jump out of your skins," Heleth's voice said. "I'm back."

But they did jump, all of them. And Cord was also startled to realize that Heleth's voice came from behind them and to one side. Then he understood. She had come back through the secondary, branching tunnel—not through the main tunnel that they had been following.

"They're not far behind me," Heleth went on quickly. "Moving fast, with lights—along this branch tunnel. Must have heard you fire the gun and were close enough to get a fix on the sound."

Lathan's voice broke in. The odd casualness was gone, and there was a crisp harshness in his words. "Then this is a good place for us to part company."

Cord stared into the darkness, as a murmur of astonishment swept through the group. "What are you talking about?" Samella demanded.

"I'm staying here," Lathan said firmly. "It's time to stop running—for me, anyway."

"But you sounded like you didn't think we could ambush the Crushers here," Jeko said.

"There might be a way," Lathan replied. "But it only needs one person." A note of urgency crept into his voice. "This was never your fight. The Crushers came to Klydor after *me*. So—they'll find me. And if I can finish them, I'll be doing a favour for you as well as for the resistance. Now get going!"

"No chance," Jeko said aggressively. "I still got this ripper, y'know. If you're stayin' to fight, so'm I. Why should you have all the fun? I'm sick of runnin', too."

"And me," Rontal and Heleth said instantly, together.

A mixture of emotions flooded through Cord—bewilderment, anxiety, and also a strange anger. Then he realized that he felt angry because he felt as Jeko did. He was weary of running, weary of the tension and fear and numbing claustrophobia. Generations of fighting Highland courage and pride flared up within him—along with his surging temper, and his undying hatred for everything that the approaching enemy stood for.

"It *is* our fight, now," he heard Samella say. "The Crushers want us as much as you. If you're going to face them, we have to help."

"That's right," Cord said hoarsely. He would have wanted Samella, above all, to be out of the near-hopeless battle that was to come. But he knew her too well to suggest it. "We're staying."

"That's stupid!" Lathan snapped. "Jeko may have a ripper-gun, but there are only two useless spears among the rest of you . . ."

"You'd have less than that if you stayed alone," Cord said angrily, cutting him off. "We'll throw rocks at them, if we have to."

"You better start collecting some," Heleth broke in sharply. "They're coming."

Cord wheeled towards her voice and blinked. It seemed at first like an illusion—but he thought that he could *see* Heleth, a vague, dark, shadowy outline. Then he realized that it was true. In the blackness behind her, deep in the twisting bowels of the secondary tunnel, there was a flicker of orange, erratic but clear.

The lights of the Crushers were advancing, steadily and menacingly, along that branch tunnel.

13

Underground
Battle

At the first glimpse of those approaching lights, the group retreated to the dubious shelter of the rock-pile. The two Streeters and Heleth had exchanged a few muted whispers—sounding almost eager, Cord thought—but now all was silent as they waited.

Cord stared unblinkingly into the darkness. He was aware of Samella's tension on one side of him, while on the other side Lathan crouched as unmoving as if carved from stone. But Cord was hot with his own wild excitement, mingled with something that felt like hunger—for battle. Whatever was going to happen, at least the time of running and hiding and waiting had ended.

Then his head jerked. The branch tunnel, several metres away, was more clearly outlined, an irregular shape of orange-red.

The Crushers were almost upon them. The lights they were carrying were reaching into the main tunnel, where Cord and the others waited.

He watched, motionless, as the light grew brighter, until the mouth of the branch tunnel was filled with a yellow glow. It seemed unnatural that the glow should be so soft and lambent and appealing—when it meant that brutal violence and death were only steps away.

Then every part of Cord's mind focused on that glow. Outlined in the tunnel mouth was the dark shape of a crouching man, the metal of a ripper-gun glinting in his hand.

As swiftly as it had appeared, the shape disappeared, as the man drew back into the branch tunnel. Cord heard the low voices of the Crushers, and the tunnel's amplifier effect carried a few of their words to his ears.

". . . Pile of rocks . . . nothin' movin' . . ."

"Wouldn't stop an' fight . . . they'd keep runnin' . . ."

"Better make sure . . ."

The dire meaning of those last three words had barely sunk into Cord's understanding when they were turned into furious, murderous action.

Two Crushers leaped with blurring speed out from the patch of yellow light, into the main tunnel. As they were in mid-leap, the lights snapped off, plunging everything back into impenetrable darkness. In the fractional second of silence that followed, Cord heard only a faint rasp, like cloth rubbing lightly against rock.

Then the ripper-guns opened up.

Invisible in the main tunnel, the two Crushers fired steadily at where they knew the rock-pile lay. The deadly mini-grenades exploded, one after another, in small fountains of splinters and shrapnel. Cord felt the stings on his back as some of the flying fragments struck him—and he pressed himself into the ground, one arm flung over Samella in a hopeless attempt to keep her from harm. More and more grenades battered at the rubble that sheltered them, and Cord heard some of the rocks rattle as they shattered or tumbled away.

Then Heleth's clear voice cut through the fury of the attack. "They're moving in! Both sides, ten metres!"

She had barely spoken when the tunnel was filled with the dazzling flare of the sun-gun. Cord recklessly raised his head and saw Lathan, up on one knee in the teeth of the grenades, firing the gun in a sweep across the tunnel.

But darkness and haste thwarted his aim. The flaming bolt from the sun-gun struck the left-hand wall of the tunnel half a metre above the head of the Crusher lurking there. And though Lathan adjusted his aim as he swung the gun to the right, the second Crusher dived with frightening speed beneath the yellow blaze, and in the same motion rolled and fired another raking burst from his ripper.

Lathan barely had time to drop back behind the rock-pile as the heavy blackness surrounded them again, and the mini-grenades erupted around him. Cord too flung himself back down, feeling a red-hot slash across his cheek as a flying shard of metal caught him.

Jeko's shout rose above the crashing explosions. "Again!"

Cord raised his head once more, as Lathan responded. The sun-gun's dazzle burst out a second time, but again seared harmlessly above the two Crushers, who were crouched low in the centre of the tunnel. Yet without any apparent time to take aim, the ripper-gun in Jeko's hand spat its soft echo of the sun-gun's blast. And as the darkness enveloped the tunnel again, Cord saw the vivid after-image of one Crusher spinning, with a cry, as Jeko's grenade tore into the flesh of one arm.

Cord dropped back, awed at the speed and accuracy of Jeko's snap-shot, in the brief flare of the sun-gun. But Jeko was not pleased.

"Just winged one," he said in a snarling whisper.

"They're moving back into the branch tunnel," Heleth said calmly.

Only then did Cord's dazed mind register the fact that the onslaught of grenades had stopped. But he had no doubt that it would begin again, soon enough.

"Probably reloading," Lathan said quietly.

"Wish I could," Jeko grumbled. "I got about six grenades left in this thing."

"This didn't work out so good, did it?" Rontal said, his voice sounding almost conversational.

"It isn't exactly what I had in mind," Lathan said cryptically.

"An ambush was always a slim chance," Samella put in. "But worth trying."

"Just doesn't leave us much choice, now," Rontal growled. "We stay here and get killed, or run for it and get killed."

"The tunnel twists and turns a lot up ahead," Heleth said. "If we made a break for it, they'd only have a clear shot at us for a few seconds."

Lathan's voice sounded weary. "They'd still come after us and hunt us down."

"Maybe," Heleth said. "But if this fight goes on too long, here, those grenades could bring the whole tunnel down on us."

Cord glanced up, automatically, though he could see nothing. He had almost forgotten, in the face of the battle, how shaky the roof of the tunnel had appeared—and how they were being sheltered by the rubble from an earlier fall.

"Then why don't you all get out of here," Lathan was saying, "like I . . ."

His voice stopped abruptly. A beam of light had suddenly reached out from the mouth of the branch tunnel, bathing the rock-pile where they crouched.

As it did so, two more Crushers sprang like flitting shadows out of the light, plunging into the blackness of the main tunnel. And once more the rock-pile was under siege.

Again they all flattened themselves, huddling against the stony ground as the mini-grenades blasted around them. But Cord had had time to see the Crusher's new strategy. One of them, standing out of sight just inside the branch tunnel, was holding his light around the wall of rock that hid him, directing its beam on to the rock-pile. The two Crushers in the main tunnel, unseen in the blackness beyond the light, could fire freely at a much more visible enemy.

The grenades flew at them so thickly that it seemed to be a continuous explosion. Cord realized that most of the Crushers' fire was being aimed at one or two weak points in the rock-pile, which were steadily being blasted open, reducing the protection for the huddled defenders. The thought chilled Cord, so that he hardly noticed the further sharp pains as more splinters of rock and shrapnel cut at him. We should have run while they were reloading, he thought with bitter fury. Now we may not get another chance.

Without warning Lathan lunged up, his silvery suit gleaming in the flaming blast of the sun-gun. The dazzling beam sprayed across the mouth of the branch tunnel, gouging huge chunks of rock from beside it. Then the beam struck the light held by the unseen Crusher, and reduced it instantly to a handful of molten metal.

In the light of the sun-gun Jeko was up and firing as well, hurling grenades back at grenades, then ducking back at the same instant as Lathan also dropped down behind the rubble.

"Think I nicked another of them," Jeko said, sounding irritated. "Didn't hurt him much."

Once again, as suddenly as it had begun, the firing of the other rippers halted.

"Can't see a thing after all that light," Heleth complained. "But it sounds like they've gone back into the branch tunnel again."

"They're in no hurry," Rontal grumbled. "Could prob'ly keep this up all day."

"Not me," Jeko snarled. "My gun's empty. And I keep thinkin' 'bout the roof."

"Then we'd better move," Samella said decisively. "Cord? Lathan?"

"All right," Cord said gloomily.

Lathan had not spoken. The others stirred in the silence, and Cord reached a hand to the man huddled invisibly beside him.

His hand encountered a warm stickiness, the unmistakeable feel of blood, drenching Lathan's suit.

"Lathan's been hit!" Cord said thickly.

Samella took a sharp breath. "We'll have to carry him. I'll take the sun-gun . . ."

But Cord was barely listening. Within his mind, some barrier had seemed to break. The fact that the ambush had failed, that Lathan was hurt or killed, that they must now begin another time of tense and probably hopeless flight, produced in him a sudden, explosive surge of fury—the mindless, savage rage of a cornered beast. For an instant he was on the verge of flinging himself, suicidally, barehanded, at the branch tunnel where the Crushers lurked. Only a supreme effort of will dragged him back from that brink. And when that struggle was won, all in a fleeting second, the ferocious rage within him had turned cold and steely, feeding his new determination.

He knew with utter clarity what had to be done, and just how to do it.

"I can't carry Lathan," he said. "My hand got cut up." He sensed Samella worriedly reaching out to him and drew back in the darkness so as not to reveal the lie. "Rontal, Jeko, you take him. I'll handle the sun-gun one-handed and come last, in case they rush us again."

"Cord . . ." Samella began doubtfully.

"*Go on!*" Cord snapped with cold ferocity.

Heleth and the two Streeters, who had obeyed orders all their lives within their gangs, jerked at the sharp edge of command. Swiftly Rontal and Jeko gathered Lathan up, muttering over the extent of his injury. Without another word, they turned away with their burden, Heleth falling in beside them to be their eyes during the retreat.

Cord could sense Samella hesitating, and his anger grew with desperation. There could be only seconds left.

"Move!" he snarled. "I'll be right behind you, and I don't want to trip over you!"

He felt Samella flinch at the rage in his voice and was aware that she had turned to join the others. With grim satisfaction, he heard the soft sound of their boots as they moved away through the blackness.

He reached around in the rubble and grasped the cool metal of the sun-gun, where it had fallen from Lathan's hands. Then he braced himself, took a deep breath, and tried to make his voice sound filled with fear, rather than with the cold battle fury that he felt.

"Run for it!" he yelled, as if the others were still there. "While we have the chance!"

The reaction was instantaneous. He heard the thud of running feet from the branch tunnel, the muffled growl of voices. He stared fixedly into the blackness, waiting, seeing only—in his mind's eye—the huge gouge that the sun-gun had made in the rock when Lathan had fired at the mouth of the other tunnel.

Then the darkness was shattered by a blaze of light. In that brightness, Cord saw the five Crushers, lights and guns in hand, advancing towards the rock-pile.

They looked confident, believing that their prey had fled, but that they would soon—as before—catch up with them. And Cord knew that they had not seen him, crouched silently in the shadows of the heap of rubble.

His finger reached for the sun-gun's firing stud. And in that last instant, he guessed that what he had in mind was probably the same thing that Lathan had intended to do, when he wanted to remain behind, alone. It was the one *sure* thing that he could do, to destroy the Crushers, without risking being killed by their guns before he could fire.

Somehow, despite his burning rage, the notion that he was stealing Lathan's plan struck him as funny. But it was not laughter that burst from his lips. It was a wild, glad, Highland battle cry, filling the tunnel at the same moment as the sun-gun's livid fire blasted forth.

The dazzling beam struck upwards, at the roof of the cave. At the slabs and lumps of rock that only precariously held up the immense weight of earth and stone above it.

And with a thunderous, tumultuous, grinding roar that sounded as if the earth itself was bellowing in rage, the entire roof of the tunnel collapsed upon them all.

14

Back from the Dead

Consciousness seeped slowly back into Cord's mind, and with it came four words that echoed hollowly inside his skull.

I am not dead.

They were the same words that had risen in his mind when he had awakened after the crash-landing on Klydor. For a moment, he felt that he was on the wrecked spaceship again—his mind just as dazed, his body throbbing as if he had been cruelly beaten.

But then he felt a waft of cool air, and his mind moved farther into wakefulness. The pain receded to a dulling ache in head and chest and vague stinging sensations over much of his skin.

He opened his eyes, staring blankly up at a clear sky. By the position of the sun, he saw that it was morning—so he had been unconscious for some hours. He stirred, and realized that he was not wearing his tunic, and that there were crude bandages on his upper body and a wrapping around his head. And then Samella's face appeared above him, concern showing in her eyes.

Cord found his voice with difficulty. "Did you . . . all make it?" he croaked.

Samella smiled. "We're all here. All in one piece."

Relief surged through Cord like an injection of adrenalin. He struggled to sit up, ignoring the pounding in his head. The others were standing around him, grinning, looking healthy enough. But their tunics were ripped and blood-stained, as if they had been clawed. The grenades, Cord realized—those rock splinters, and shrapnel. And the stinging all over his body was from the same thing.

He saw with surprise that they were back in the shallow basin, next to the shiny mass of the CeeDee spaceship. The airlock of the ship stood open, just as it had been when Cord had last seen it—which seemed years before.

"Lathan?" he asked, not looking forward to the answer.

But again he was surprised. "He made it too," Samella said. "He lost some flesh at his side, but we stopped the bleeding and patched him up." She glanced disapprovingly at the spaceship. "He's weak, but he won't rest. He's in the ship, rummaging around."

"Lookin' for stuff we can use," Rontal said.

Samella nodded grudgingly. "Especially a medi-kit. We've used up everything we had."

Cord reached up to touch the thick bandage around his head. "Tell me what happened . . . in the tunnel."

Samella turned her look of disapproval on to him. "You know what happened. You sent us off and stayed behind to get killed."

"Real noble," Jeko said, grinning.

"Heroic," Heleth said sarcastically.

"When we heard your yell," Samella went on, "and then the collapse of the tunnel, we went back. And, thanks to Heleth's eyes, we dug you out."

"The whole roof came down, but nothing heavy hit you," Heleth said. "Just dirt and rubble. The big rocks and stuff fell only a little ways from you—the tunnel's blocked solid." She peered at Cord with a shade of anxiety. "The Crushers were *in* the tunnel, weren't they?"

Cord nodded. "All five of them. They were coming at me when I fired at the roof."

"Crushers got crushed," Jeko said gleefully.

"And you've got a lump on your head as big as a fist," Samella said severely, "and probably some cracked ribs. But I don't suppose you'll stay still any more than Bren will."

"I'll mend just as well standing up as lying down," Cord said. He got slowly to his feet, trying not to grimace at the renewed pounding in his head, the stab of fire in his chest. And then they all turned, as a cheery shout came from the spaceship.

Bren Lathan stood in the open airlock. His silvery jumpsuit was filthy, ragged and stained with dried blood. His face was pale, and he had a thickly wadded bandage covering one side. But he was grinning and holding up a small metal case.

"Look what I found!" he said.

Samella's eyes lit up. "GUIDE!"

"Thank you for activating me," said the soft voice of the little computer.

Cord found himself grinning with delight. It was like meeting an old friend after a long parting.

"Give me a hand," Lathan said. "There's plenty of stuff—a full medi-kit, food, lots of supplies."

"How 'bout a few sun-guns?" Jeko asked hopefully.

Lathan smiled. "No weapons. The Crushers must have had only the sun-guns and rippers."

"It doesn't matter," Samella said. "We don't need more guns, now." She glanced at Cord. "We found the sun-gun, too, when we dug you out. It's still working, good as new."

Cord looked round and saw the heavy weapon leaning against a small heap of boulders. For an instant he felt cold and shaky as he recalled those final seconds in the tunnel, with the gun in his hands, waiting for the moment to fire, to bury his enemies and himself in order to save his friends. Then the coldness faded, and he felt again the surge of relief and joy. They were all alive—even GUIDE—with no enemies to threaten them, with fresh supplies, with the whole planet awaiting them as before.

By the expressions on the others' faces, they felt the same way. They went to join Lathan in the ship, staring curiously at the roomy interior, the gleaming equipment and the intricate control panel. Somewhere, Cord knew, stored out of sight, would be the corpse of the sixth Crusher—the one killed by a beaked monster in the caves. But no one mentioned that as they set to work. Samella cast a longing glance at the splendid computer forming the heart of the ship's controls, but she did her share as they unloaded what they needed from the ship's supplies. They even found some light, colourful, sleeveless shirts to replace their torn and stained tunics. And there were some well-made backpacks in simu-leather to carry everything in.

Soon they had taken a sizeable stack of supplies out of the ship, stowing them among the cluster of rocks where the sun-gun lay. And when the last item was placed on the pile, Cord asked the question that was on everyone's mind.

"What now?" he said. He was looking especially at Bren Lathan.

Lathan shrugged. "Rest here awhile, get over our wounds, then—see what happens. Have you got any plans?"

There was something different about the way he spoke, Cord thought. And then he realized. Lathan was no longer talking to them as an adult speaks to teenagers. He was talking to them as friends and equals.

Samella looked thoughtful. "We'll get back to what we were doing before—exploring the planet, looking for a place to make a home."

The others nodded in agreement.

"I suppose you'll be leaving," Samella went on, to Lathan. "But before then we'd still like to know more about the rebellion, or whatever it is."

Again the others agreed, with eagerness.

"I'll tell you, of course," Lathan said readily. "But there's no hurry. I'm not going anywhere."

Samella frowned. "But you have this ship. You could get to another planet—to your friends . . ."

"Not on this ship," Lathan told her. "I couldn't take it off Klydor. As soon as I got into space, CeeDee headquarters on Earth would contact it—and they'd know I wasn't Warreck. So they'd send out other ships, to come after me. It'd start all over again."

By then Rontal was frowning too. "There's a thought," he said. "Maybe Warreck already reported back—'bout you, and us, and everythin'."

"No," Lathan assured him. "A ship can't communicate with other planets while it's on the ground. The gravitational field prevents it. The Crushers would have had to lift off, get into deep space, to send a message. And they didn't."

They all looked relieved—until Cord thought of something else. "The ship is still a problem," he said. "It'll be a giveaway, when the ColSec inspectors come, a few months from now . . ."

"I can fix that," Lathan said. "As far as the ColSec inspectors will know, I landed here in my escape module, all by myself, quite innocently."

"How'll you *fix* it?" Heleth wanted to know.

"I'll show you," Lathan said. "But you'll have to move away from the ship."

Curious and interested, the teenagers began to move away. "Bet he blows it up," Jeko said eagerly. Cord glanced over at their stack of supplies and saw that it was well protected from an explosion, tucked away behind the boulders. And he was safely carrying GUIDE, in one of the new backpacks—though carrying the pack in one hand, not strapped over the painful cuts and bruises on his back.

Samella was looking worriedly back at Lathan. "I still think you should rest. The ship can wait."

"I'm all right," Lathan said. "You go ahead—it won't take long."

107

The teenagers continued to withdraw, as Lathan turned to the ship. Then they all stopped, with a jolting suddenness as if they had run into a wall.

A voice had spoken, from within the shadow cast by the ship. A choked, hoarse voice, filled with fury and murder.

"Nobody's goin' anywhere," the voice said.

Cord hardly recognized what he saw. It was a man, but one who looked more dead than alive. His clothing was shredded, so that the powerful upper body was nearly naked. And the ragged clothing and bare flesh seemed drenched with blood. There was also just as much blood as sweat-streaked dirt that formed the hideous mask of his face. But the glaring eyes, the thin twisted mouth, the rasping voice, were all those of the Crusher captain, Warreck.

And though Warreck was swaying, as if at the end of his physical resources, he was gripping the laserifle as steadily as ever.

"Thought I was dead," he snarled. "Like the others. But it takes more'n a few rocks to kill me. Takes more'n a few snake-monsters, in the dark. Takes more'n any of you blanks got."

Cord stared, silent and numb. Somehow Warreck, too, had escaped the full impact of the crushing fall of rock. Somehow he had fought his way out of the tunnels—through the night, when the blade-beaked horrors were active. Somehow he had survived it all, had even held on to the laserifle, and had come back to claim his ship—and his vengeance.

From the corner of his eye Cord saw the two Streeters, faces calm and expressionless, begin to move. Gradually, a centimetre at a time, they edged away from the group—spreading out, Cord realized, so the Crusher could not cut them all down with a single sweep of the laser.

But Warreck, his blazing eyes fixed on Bren Lathan, did not seem to notice. Carefully, Cord also began to move. He knew that the sun-gun lay among the boulders, far too many steps away. They were all empty-handed—though Cord still held GUIDE, in the backpack. He had no idea what anyone could do. But he knew that they could not simply stand there and let Warreck kill them.

"Now you and me, Lathan," Warreck was saying, "we're gonna fly away. You can come alive or dead."

He gestured jerkily with the rifle, indicating that Lathan should enter the ship. Cord tensed, aware that the others were also poising themselves.

"It's all right," Lathan said quietly. He was looking at Warreck, but Cord knew that he was speaking to the group of teenagers. "Don't do anything. It's me he wants."

"Wrong," Warreck grated. "I want all of you. But I'm not stupid enough to think I can guard six people and fly a ship." Again he jerked the rifle. "C'mon, Lathan. Slow and easy."

Coolly, Lathan stepped towards the ship, with Warreck behind him. The others moved warily after them, but halted as Warreck swung the rifle in their direction. Slowly he backed away, keeping both Lathan and the teenagers in view. Then he turned and thrust Lathan through the airlock with a savage push.

"Get the engines started, Lathan," Warreck rasped. "And no tricks. You try anythin', I kill the kids." He turned his glare towards the teenagers.

Cord's mind was racing, trying desperately to work out some way of saving Lathan. He could see the same desperation on the faces of the others. It occurred to him that Lathan could simply close the airlock, even lift off. But then Warreck would carry out his threat, and the teenagers knew that Lathan would not leave them to die.

"You dulls can wait," Warreck was saying, with an evil grin. "You're not goin' anywhere. And when I get Lathan where he's goin', I'll be back, with a team, and hunt you down."

Cord heard the words, but he was not looking at Warreck. His gaze had shifted to the rear of the spaceship, where slender plumes of flame had appeared, accompanied by a deep, throbbing rumble. The mighty engines had started up and were building their power.

Warreck moved carefully to the airlock, the laserifle still rigid in his hands. The rumble of the engines was rising into a bellow, but the hoarse voice was audible above it.

"Run and hide, kids," Warreck snarled. "Won't do you any good. I'll find you." The wild glare settled on Cord. "I said you'd be a long time dyin'. Count on it."

Then he stepped back, framed for a instant in the open airlock. In that instant, Rontal launched himself forward.

The laserifle swung towards him, and the beam lanced out. Cord glimpsed Rontal diving forward and down, avoiding the beam. But by then Cord too was moving.

The rolling muscles of his shoulder and arm seemed to gain extra power from anger and desperation. He flung the backpack containing GUIDE, like a rocket, at the snarling face of Warreck.

It struck with a meaty thud, dropping into the airlock. And Warreck toppled backwards into the ship, the rifle falling from his hands.

"Lathan!" Cord yelled, as he and the others leaped forward.

Lathan appeared in the airlock, ashen-faced, wild-eyed. "Stay back!" he shouted. As they halted, he bent to scoop up both GUIDE and the laserifle, then leaped from the ship and sprinted towards the teenagers.

Behind him, the airlock slid shut. The thunder of the engines had risen to an ear-shattering howl. The ship trembled, seeming to poise itself. Then, majestically, it began to rise on a spreading tower of flame.

Cord watched dejectedly as the ship carried their enemy into the sky. "Wish you'd thrown something that killed him," Heleth said savagely. "Now he'll be back for sure."

"He won't be," Lathan said flatly.

"How can you be sure?" Samella asked.

"Because I was never going to let him take me back alive," Lathan said. "He'd use me to finish the resistance. So when I was starting the engines, I rigged a by-pass in the power cut-off. The engines will reach overload—very soon."

The others stared at him. Then they all looked up to watch the ship, climbing swiftly and steadily, dwindling in size. In seconds it was no more than a bright, speeding dot in the sky.

And they watched without the slightest change of expression as the bright dot suddenly expanded into a blazing yellow bloom of flame and destruction.

15

Rebels

"So," Lathan said, "the CeeDees will know only that a team of Crushers went into space looking for rebels, and were never heard from again. An unexplained mystery. There's lots of those, in space."

The six of them were sprawled on the ground in the place where they had been when the fiery flower in the sky had signalled the end of Warreck and the CeeDee ship. All of them had been silent for some time, almost stupefied. Yet Cord felt excited as well as dazed—because in the wake of their unbelievable victory, they could actually start thinking again about the future, on Klydor. And part of his excitement came from the feeling that their future might be somewhat different from the one that they had planned before.

"And when the ColSec inspectors land," Samella said, following up Lathan's remark, "they'll find that Bren Lathan, famous space explorer, hadn't disappeared in some other unexplained mystery, but is safe on Klydor."

"Right," Lathan said, grinning. "They'll give me another ship and send me out to work again."

"On that subject," Samella said, "will you tell us now about your *other* work? The rebellion you're leading?"

Lathan held up a hand. "It's not really a rebellion," he said. "And I'm not really the leader . . ."

"Don't tell us what's not," Heleth broke in firmly. "Tell us what *is*."

And the five teenagers settled themselves to listen, as Lathan began.

He reminded them that ColSec had placed many colonies on suitable planets around the galaxy. And all of them had been peopled by young outlaws, mainly from the gangs of Earth's inner cities, the wild teenagers who refused to obey the restrictions imposed on the rest of Earth.

Many of the colonies had been established for years, and the colonists had grown older and more numerous. They had found valuable resources on their worlds, so that considerable wealth was flowing from them to Earth, to ColSec and the Organization. But none of the colonists had ever forgotten their bitter hatred for those on Earth who had so ruthlessly condemned them to permanent exile.

Cord nodded grimly at that. He knew for himself that the flame of hatred for ColSec would burn within him for the rest of his life.

So the colonies, Lathan went on, were a natural growing ground for rebellion—especially since the wild young people on those planets now lived a long way from the repressive power of the Organization and its Civil Defenders.

"There are small CeeDee detachments on a few of the older colonies," Lathan said. "But that's all. I suppose ColSec thought that the hardships of alien worlds would keep the kids too busy to start trouble. But ColSec was wrong. There's been trouble for many years."

At first, he said, it was vague and undirected. The resources of a planet might be hidden, or damaged, so that ColSec never received them. "Accidents" might happen to ColSec inspectors, or CeeDee investigators. Occasional ships—Cord and his friends grinned at this remark—might vanish mysteriously in space.

"But they were all one-off operations," Lathan said. "There was

113

no way for one colony to know what another one was doing. Not till I got involved."

Lathan had been wild enough in his own youth, he told them, and had narrowly avoided ending up as just another young criminal. And he had never lost the yearning to break out of the dull, fearful, repressed life that most people lived on Earth. So he became a space explorer, out in the reaches of the galaxy, far from the grip of the Organization.

And, in his wanderings through space, he saw the simmering rebellion that existed within each of ColSec's colonies. And he saw that he was in a special position to be of use to the rebellion and help it grow.

"What I am," he told his enthralled audience, "is a communications link. So are some other explorers—we're all much alike, choosing this kind of work to get away from Earth and the Organization. We're slowly bringing the colonies together, organizing and planning the resistance, as a united force."

But as they did so, he added, they began running more and more risks.

"At last, somebody got careless," he said bleakly, "and ColSec got wind of what's happening. That's why the Crushers came out—looking for rebels and rebel leaders." He shook his head. "They raided a meeting I was at, and I nearly didn't get away. I got to my ship just a jump ahead of them—and even then they disabled my ship, so that it blew up some time later, and I had to use the escape module. And they trailed me here—though they still hadn't identified me."

"Do you think there'll be more Crushers, looking for the rebels now?" Samella asked.

"Probably," Lathan said. "As the resistance gets going, things will get more dangerous. If we become too much of a nuisance, in an organized way, ColSec won't send six Crushers. They'll send an army. And then the resistance will become a war."

Jeko's eyes gleamed at that, but Rontal frowned. "What'll you fight with?" he asked.

"We're gathering weapons," Lathan said. "We even have a few spaceships—some of those that got 'lost' in space. If it comes to fighting, we'll fight."

"Do you really think you can win?" Samella asked.

Lathan shrugged. "We don't have any wild ideas about freeing Earth from the rule of the Organization. That's probably an impossible dream. But every one of the colonies on other planets has a special dream that may *be* possible. To get out from under ColSec's control. To be a place where people can run their own lives—self-governing, and free."

He glanced around, seeing the light in the eyes of his five listeners. "I think you know what I mean," he continued quietly. "I also think that you can play a very special part in this . . . rebellion."

"Sure," Heleth said sourly. "You tell those other colonies that there're five kids on Klydor with spears and clubs who're ready to fight ColSec. They'll think the war's as good as won."

Lathan laughed. "Maybe not. But I don't underrate you five—not now. The fact that you survived at all, with almost no supplies, is nearly a miracle. So is the fact that all six of us are still here, today. It means that you're unusually tough, and smart, and *lucky*. And that you have some special abilities, too." He grinned at Heleth. "But you've got something else that could be very valuable to the resistance. You've got Klydor."

His grin widened at their puzzled expressions. "This is a good planet," he continued. "It's got more to offer than almost any of the other colony planets—including huge areas that can support human life in real comfort and safety. You could transplant half of Earth to Klydor, and they could all live here happily."

"What are you getting at?" Cord asked uneasily.

"I'm saying that Klydor could be a *base* for the resistance," Lathan

115

said. "Which is something we need. Understand, we don't want to go to war with ColSec if we can avoid it. We want to try to convince them that it would be too *costly* for them to set out to crush us. We want to show them that they'd do better to let us have our freedom and learn to . . . co-exist with us."

"How do you do that?" Samella asked.

"By showing them the *expense* they'd face," Lathan replied. "That's a language they understand. Fighting a long-distance war on other planets could cripple them, if it went on for long. And we could undermine them even more by cutting off the flow of resources from the colonies. We'd threaten to *close down the colonies*—and to use our ships to ferry the colonists to another place. To Klydor."

Cord's excitement grew as he thought about it. It would be a serious threat to ColSec. The profits from the colonies were crucial to the impoverished Earth. And it would be hugely expensive for ColSec to rebuild the colonies it had already set up. It might work, he thought. We might *buy* our freedom, by threatening to cut off ColSec's lifeline.

But, as ever, Samella's clear intelligence saw a flaw. "All ColSec would have to do, then," she pointed out, "would be to send its army to Klydor and take it over. End of rebellion."

"Perhaps," Lathan said calmly. "But we have a plan that would face ColSec with the task of fighting a very long, and very costly, guerrilla war, if they attacked Klydor. Even ColSec might think twice about starting that fight."

"What plan?" the others asked, as one.

"We recruit an army of our own," Lathan said intensely. "Secretly, and slowly. We recruit an army of people who know all about guerrilla warfare. And we bring them here, to Klydor, before ColSec even knows what's happening."

The teenagers sat in stunned silence, hardly able to take it all in. Just a few days before, they had been concerned with nothing but peacefully wandering around their world. And now they were on the threshold of being plunged into the midst of a rebellion, and perhaps an interplanetary war.

"ColSec'll find out," Rontal said. "They'll stop you 'fore you get goin'."

Lathan shook his head. "It only needs a few people to recruit this army and get it here. And if it works, the army will be here and in place before ColSec can mobilize a force against it. Except by then, they might not think it's worthwhile to do so."

Samella looked at him, realization dawning in her eyes. "Just a few people, you said . . ."

"Right," Lathan agreed. "I see you know who I mean. This plan never got going before because the rebels hadn't found a place to set up their base, and were worried about the risks. But now those problems are solved." His grin was fierce. "Klydor is the ideal place. And you people are the ideal recruiters for the special army."

"Why us?" Jeko asked.

"Because you already know Klydor," Lathan said. "Because you're tough and smart and lucky. Because none of you would betray one another. And because as far as ColSec knows, you don't *exist*. You died on this wild planet, after your crash-landing."

"They'll know about us," Cord pointed out, "when their inspectors come here."

"There are ways around that," Lathan said. "We have time to work it all out—like the details of how to recruit an army under the nose of the Organization."

"And where do we go looking for this army?" Heleth asked. "The other colonies?"

Lathan shook his head. "We don't want to shift the other colonists unless we have to. If we do start bringing them here, we'll need an army already in place, to keep ColSec from attacking Klydor."

"Then where . . ." Cord began. But he stopped, seeing the

117

answer. And the others went silent as well, making the same realization.

"You find the army where ColSec found you," Lathan said quietly. "Where you all started from. On Earth."

The five teenagers looked at one another, knowing that their lives were about to change again, in a way as far-reaching and frightening as the immense change that had exiled them to Klydor. All of them realized clearly the incredible risks they would run, the daunting odds against their success. But there was a fire in their eyes, the glint of willingness and determination and wild courage.

They could be the spearhead of a movement that might lead many thousands of other young people to freedom. The prospect was terrifying—and irresistible.

Cord smiled slowly, and his friends returned the smile. "It looks," he said at last, "like we'll be going home for a while."